Tried and True

A THRESHOLD SERIES PREQUEL

YAHAVIM

"God gave you life; live for Him.
He gave you strength; learn its limits.
He gave you songs; sing evermore."

Tried and True

P rissie asked, "Will you tell me about your girl … lady?"

Taweel nodded and said, "My charge was a girl, born thousands of years ago in Egypt."

"Was she pretty?"

He considered her question and eventually answered, "Her hair was dark, her eyes were light, and she was fond of cats."

—Threshold Series, Book 4, *The Garden Gate*

Introduction

Introduction

ried and True is a small story with small chapters, set many centuries before Prissie Pomeroy's adventure in *The Blue Door*. In the Threshold Series, Prissie is privileged to meet the two angels that serve as her Guardians. This is the story of the path that eventually brought them to her, beginning during Taweel's apprenticeship.

I originally shared *Tried and True* on my blog as a serial, with new chapters posted weekdaily. Short and sweet, each installment is exactly 100 words long. A creative challenge for me, a quick story-burst for readers who followed along. I hope you'll find your way onto my website as well. There's always something new.

The timeline for this serial predates the other books and stories I've written about the Pomeroys. However, the sharp-eyed reader will find cameos and cross-references. New details are revealed. Future storylines are foreshadowed. During the writing of this serial, I introduced three (fictional) angelic orders—the Weavers, the Forgers, and the Fourfold—and set the stage for another serial: *Sage and Song*.

While this story holds its own, I'd recommend starting with the Threshold Series. That way, you'll catch all the allusions and better appreciate the tension that's building between two angelic "brothers." The main series is complete in four volumes, and the list of companion stories continues to grow. You'll find more details and summaries at the end of this e-book. And as always, I chat about my latest authorial news at ChristaKinde.com.

But for now, join Taweel on the darkest night of his life.

CHRISTA KINDE

1

Every Firstborn Child

Another scream. Pleading denials. Waves of despair. Taweel knelt on the roof of a merchant's dwelling, too numb to respond to the uproar. Hundreds upon thousands of Guardians were similarly bereft, but knowing he wasn't alone didn't lessen the shock.

She'd been so *young*.

Broken voices. Frightened pleas. Quavering dirges. Their gods might be false, but their sorrow was as real as Taweel's. He covered his face as the girl's tenderhearted father choked on his sobs, and her mother cursed the prince who had betrayed Egypt.

The tenth plague would set God's children free, but it cost Taweel his charge.

2
Past Tense

Taweel had known nothing but dread since the announcement of the final plague. The girl whose name God had placed under his hand had suffered so much. Thirst. Fleas. Frogs. But especially the darkness. "She is afraid of the dark."

"Come away." Dorum laid a hand on his apprentice's broad shoulder. "She is no longer here. Your service has ended"

"I know." Taweel's voice broke, and a sob escaped his tight throat. The child he loved had suffered … and died.

"There are next things to consider."

"No." Taweel dragged shaking purple wings closer to the shrouded pallet. "Not yet."

3
NEXT THINGS

Shortly after dawn, Dorum managed to interrupt Taweel's brooding. "There have been new assignments in nearly every Flight. The exodus will scatter us all."

Taweel glanced up to find theirs gathered and quickly lowered his gaze.

Their captain spoke into the silence. "A final song before parting … and …."

Dorum knelt and said, "Look at me, Taweel."

He obediently lifted dull purple eyes.

"You *know* what I must do."

"I am to be pierced."

"Yes. By my own hand," his mentor acknowledged. "Are you prepared?"

Taweel whispered, "It hurts."

Dorum touched the ring in his own ear. "I know."

4
PIERCED

While their Flight tightened ranks, Dorum set the point of a thornlike blade against his apprentice's left earlobe. "Their Fall followed our Fall, yet we cannot lead them into faithfulness," he recited. "We can only be Faithful, trusting Him who is Faithful."

Amidst a mournful chorus, Taweel felt a tug … a prick … a push … *pain*. Blood welled up as Dorum widened the hole enough to accept a ring. Light dimmed. Colors faded. Notes soured. The newly-pierced Guardian was shutting down so fast, he missed his mentor's news.

"We are recalled to heaven, Taweel. We can go home."

5

SQUARE ONE

Following Dorum, Taweel shot up through a ring of stones in the floor of a pavilion. Details filtered through his funk. Warm stone. God's light. The clatter and clack of Weavers' looms. The spicy scent of candle-trees. The flicker and dart of yahavim. This was the threshold of heaven. The very place Taweel had trained as a boy. Home.

"The Weavers must be delighted," Dorum remarked. "So much change. So much news."

Trudging along beside his mentor, Taweel tuned out the pleasant mingling of voices—greetings, laughter, conversation, song. He was back at the beginning, except he couldn't start over.

6
SHELTER THE INNOCENT

Taweel recalled seeing newly pierced Guardians when he was a boy. He'd hung back while other hadarim comforted returnees with haggard faces and hollow eyes. Should he have paid more attention to the possibility of sorrow?

Within the training grounds, they passed youngsters flocked around a weapons master. Several boys glanced his way, and Taweel's innards turned.

They were so *young*.

These boys needed to be strong … to hold onto fragile hopes … to succeed where he'd failed. By the time Dorum reached the tent assigned to them, Taweel had made up his mind. He needed to get away.

GAP IN THE HEDGE

Taweel followed Dorum into a tent with loose sides billowing in soft breezes. Unbuckling the sword that hung between his shoulder blades, he sat on one of two low cots. Dorum tossed his own weapon onto the other cot. "I need to speak to the overseer. Coming?"

"No."

Once his mentor stepped out, Taweel inched his sword from it sheath, stopping partway. As he feared, his charge's name was gone. Wiped from the gleaming blade as if it had never been there. With quiet deliberation, he removed his breastplate and unwound crisscrossing bootstraps. Abandoning all his gear, Taweel walked out.

8
FEELING ALONE

Guardians were quiet, focused individuals famed for their courage in the face of impossible odds. But their order's defining characteristic was bashfulness. Shy of strangers. Slow to speak. Skittish in crowds. Taweel drew curious glances, but no one stepped into his path or called him back. They left him alone.

Alone.

So much was missing, and Taweel felt his lack. No charge. No mentor. No purpose. His bare feet felt strange on stone. His hands felt empty without his sword. And for the first time in his life, he couldn't form his thoughts into a song.

And that felt wrong.

The training camp's overseer approached Dorum. "Where is Taweel?"

"I do not know."

"Your own apprentice?" Valerian asked in surprise.

Dorum slowly drew his sword and displayed the barren blade. "His name is no longer under my hand. But his grief is mine as well."

Valerian frowned. "Is he in danger?"

"Taweel's heart was deeply pierced." Gazing into the arching branches of a candle-tree, Dorum said, "But the heart that was tender toward the child is just as tender toward the Creator. I cannot imagine his Fall."

"I have said the same," Valerian cautioned. "Sorrow can lead to greater sorrows."

10
Endless

Without a Sending, no clear path lay before Taweel. But even in unfamiliar territory some things remained the same. Wide streets. Peaceful gardens. Squat pedestals in the circles where Worshipers sang through the watches. Orderly encampments for training young cherubim and hadarim.

No matter how many streams Taweel crossed, he found no end. Eternity's vastness didn't trouble him, but he found himself looking over his shoulder … peering into strangers' faces … and even searching the sky. No pursuit. No questions. No recognition. With a grunt, he lowered his gaze and plodded on.

Some who were lost stayed that way.

11
MISTAKEN IDENTITY

No matter how long he traveled, Taweel found he couldn't walk away from his sorrow. Instead, it lay in wait for him. Rounding a corner, he came up behind a young Observer with long, dark hair. The passing resemblance to Taweel's charge jolted him into action. Whispering her name, he grabbed for the sword he no longer carried.

But it wasn't her. Because she was gone. And by the time the rattled Guardian remembered, he'd already made a spectacle of himself, standing in the middle of the road with dimming wings flung wide.

Startled looks. Sympathetic glances.

Stricken, Taweel fled.

12
SEEKER

Once he realized he was seeking a dark corner, Taweel knew he'd become too used to dwelling on earth. Here in the heavenlies, shadows were scarce. But he wanted a place to hide from searching looks and the kindness of strangers.

Lured by the trickle of water, he wandered into a garden and dropped to the low rim of a fountain. Elbows on knees, head in hands, he stared unseeing at the warm gold of paving stones. When bare feet stepped into view, Taweel blinked several times, but there was nothing wrong with his eyes. Those feet had six toes.

13
THE WEAVER

"I will hide you."

The voice was warm as light and gentle as a breeze, but Taweel's ears caught the underlying strength of purpose. This angel was Sent. To him.

He slowly lifted his gaze to find a Weaver standing there, a quizzical expression on his brown face. Taweel was just as surprised. Since when did a Weaver stop working? But then … an unarmed, unarmored hadarim was equally preposterous.

When Taweel didn't reply, the Weaver picked up the slack. "Come out of the street. Rest a while in my garden." Offering both hands, he repeated, "I will hide you."

14
TWIST AND TURN

Glancing over his shoulder, the Weaver said, "Not far now."

Taweel towered over his host, a slim angel whose ears came to neat points and whose gliding steps led unerringly along winding streets. Like all members of his order, the Weaver's hair was arranged in loops and braids, knotted with lengths of dyed cloth and ribbons. Taweel had heard that they told a tale if you knew how to read the patterns. So skillful was the arrangement, he couldn't tell if the Weaver's hair was blue or white. Not that it mattered.

All Taweel wanted was the promised hiding place.

15

HIDING PLACE

The Weaver's home was nothing like the tents used by hadarim. Stone columns and archways. Sheer curtains as vivid as angel wings. Open ceilings overhung by flowering vines. And the promised garden, where water trickled into the basin of a modest fountain.

Parting the hangings in front of an inner alcove, Taweel's host indicated a sturdy cot. "Most avoid this area for the very reason you seek it. May our oddity be of comfort."

High walls and heavy vines didn't bring darkness into this corner of heaven. But it *was* shade.

Taweel eased past the Weaver into the shadowy niche.

16
Two Novelties

Taweel lay on the cot, staring at overhead vines. Light played at the edges of his sanctuary—gently glowing, softly calling, never intruding.

"You should eat," murmured the Weaver.

He shrugged off the suggestion. He wasn't hungry. He wasn't anything.

"Sing with me."

"… I have no song."

Nimble fingers flew as the Weaver added intricate stitching to the hem of a tunic. "What novelties! Shadows *and* silence!"

There was a busyness to this angel's quiet—steadily working, willingly patient, ever present.

Taweel gruffly asked, "Why are you here?"

His host smiled. "It's not good for you to be alone."

17

IN BETWEEN

The Weaver kept busy, but Taweel ignored his comings and goings … until the angel presented him with new clothes.

"These will suit you better. Change."

Although refusal was on his lips, Taweel's interest was caught. Sitting up, he carefully accepted them. Unlike the raiment traditionally worn by warriors, this tunic had long, full sleeves. And usually, a wide band of geometric stitching indicated everything from an angel's name and order to his rank and file within the armies of heaven. "Blank?" Taweel asked.

"As a new-formed's." The Weaver spread wide his hands. "Ends. Beginnings. You're caught in the in-between."

18
NOT ALONE

Fading into the background. Gathering dust in the corner.

Taweel let half-lidded eyes drift out of focus, for he had no wish to join a dream. Curled on his side with his face to the wall, his thoughts had taken a morose turn.

Wasting valuable space. Dimming away in shadows.

His host had gone on some errand, cutting Taweel's one tie to another life. With a darkening scowl, the Guardian decided that the whole "not alone" thing had been as short-lived as his sweet charge. But then a soft *shuff* jerked Taweel's attention back to his surroundings.

He wasn't alone.

19

EYES AND EARS

Taweel turned over and stared hard at the door, automatically tensed to defend … what? His cot?

With a grunt, he flopped back onto his bed and waited for the culprit to show himself. Delicate brown fingers stirred the sheer curtains. Dark eyes with thick lashes peered through the gap. Twisting braids. Pointed ears. The boy was definitely a Weaver. And curious.

"Who are you?" Taweel asked.

The question was all the invitation the young angel needed. He hurried over to confide, "I'm Weft. Loris is my mentor."

Taweel grunted again. So the Weaver had a name. And an apprentice.

20
BLANK CANVAS

Two by two. That's how the ranks of heaven were organized. Whenever the newly-formed were brought in, each youngster was paired off with an older, wiser angel of their order for training. Taweel could remember being a child. Vaguely. But he had no idea what to say to one. Especially an inquisitive Weaver.

Weft plucked at his sleeve and asked, "Don't you have a name?"

"I do."

"Is it a secret?"

"I am Taweel." He touched his tunic's unadorned collar, which revealed nothing about his former place. "Your mentor gave me empty raiment."

"Not empty," argued Weft. "This is *ready*."

CHANGING OF THE GUARD

"**N**ot yet?"

The boy was entirely too optimistic. *Yet* implied a future in which Taweel might leave this shadowed haven. But he couldn't think of a single reason to emerge. "Go without me."

Disappointment filled Weft's eyes. "Again?"

Would the boy ever give up asking? Taweel simply shook his head.

Before Weft's patter was entirely gone, Loris's approaching steps met Taweel's ears. The changing of the guard. Except … the Weaver was running. Suddenly, a splotch of brightness hit the filmy curtain that hung across Taweel's alcove. Loris caught up and caged the buzzing, squeaking intruder between both hands. "Gotcha!"

22
HOLD STILL

Loris sat and showed off his captive. "This bit of curiosity flew too close to the skeins of dyed thread Weft and I hung out earlier. Keep him still for me?"

Taweel's hand felt over-large and clumsy as he gingerly took the yahavim between his thumb and forefinger. The tiny manna-maker hummed an unhappy note. Angels of this order might not be capable of speech, but this one showed enough sense to accept the Weaver's help freeing his delicate wings.

"Where is his shepherd?"

Faceted eyes blinked up at him.

"This one is wild," murmured Loris.

Taweel grunted. "It shows."

23
SLIP

Taweel scrutinized the sun-bright angel hanging limp in his grasp. Pointed ears poked through long yellow hair. Small hands pushed against his knuckles, then balled into fists. The yahavim gazed up at him with a pout. It was such a childish expression. Innocent. Injured. And perhaps justified. But before Taweel could apologize for his unkind remark, Loris lifted away the last loop of sapphire thread.

The little manna-maker wriggled free and darted straight up through the tumble of overhead vines. Taweel stretched out a hand, but the little one was gone without a backward glance.

He was too late. Again.

24
Meaning

"Why am I here?" Taweel sighed.

Loris glanced up from the complex pattern of sea-green thread he was embroidering onto a pant cuff. "Because you refuse to leave."

"I meant … why did you offer me this place?"

"My alcove needed brightening."

There was no denying that raiment had an inherent glow. And for the first time, it occurred to the Guardian to ask, "Why?"

"Some answers belong to God alone."

Taweel shook his head, for this was a new question. "I meant … why does raiment shine?"

Loris's smile widened. "For *that* answer, you need only ask a Weaver."

25
Six Fingers

Messengers carried messages. Protectors protected. Each order did their part, but Taweel only knew his own. "Weavers weave cloth … sew raiment." He searched his mind. "And you have six digits."

Loris held out a hand, displaying the secret to every Weaver's dexterity. It was as if the thumb and first two fingers were mirrored, doubling each hand's usefulness. Having two thumbs allowed Loris to stitch with two needles at once. "If you're curious, I could mentor you."

Taweel grunted and turned his face to the wall.

"On second thought," Loris said in serious tones. "We'll apprentice you to Weft."

26
TRADE SECRETS

Weft seemed puzzled. "You want to become a Weaver?"

"No, but I have questions only a Weaver can answer."

"Ask me!"

Taweel repeated the question he'd put to Loris earlier. "Why does raiment shine?"

The boy tipped his head to one side and recited, "A child of light walks in the light. Light sings through his veins. Light buoys his flight. Light touches his lips with sweetness. Light clothes him in radiance."

The Guardian looked more closely at his tunic's fine weave. "But where do Weavers find threads of light?"

Weft held a finger to his lips, then pointed upward.

27
FALLING LEAVES

Taweel gazed into the vines overhead, which rustled softly. What he'd taken for breezes turned out to be three of the little manna-makers. A leaf drifted down, soon followed by another. "What are they doing?"

"Yahavim do not like shadows. They are making way for more light." Leaning closer, Weft confided, "And they are looking for me."

The warrior brushed loose leaves from his shoulders. "Why is that?"

Weft lifted his hands in cheerful welcome. "I am their shepherd."

"And why would a Weaver tame a flock?" prompted Taweel, for he knew something was afoot.

The boy giggled. "For thread!"

28
STEP LADDER

Weft begged a favor, which was as close to a Sending as Taweel had known since his return. The sense of purpose was nice, even if it was a humble one. Bracing the boy's legs, he steadied the young Weaver as he twisted and tied vines into open circles. In each of these living wreaths, he hung a small bell.

With a flick of his finger, Weft tested each wee chime. High, sweet notes created an open chord that Taweel found pleasant. "Now what?" he asked.

The boy held his finger to his lips once more, then whispered, "Wait. Watch."

29
TING

Leaves stirred. Shadows shifted across the wall. Soft *ting*s lent a whisper of music to Taweel's dim alcove. The only other sound was the slip of thread through cloth as Loris added the finishing touches to a cuff.

Taweel stared absently into the greenery. He'd waited through several watches, but whatever was supposed to happen … hadn't. Still, he clung to his young mentor's instructions. Wait. Watch.

Wings fluttered. Small feet touched down inside one wreath, sending it swinging. The yahavim jumped to the second, then settled in the third, humming happily.

Loris was smiling when he remarked, "It begins."

30
TRICK OF THE LIGHT

The yahavim took his time getting comfortable—wings folded, feet tucked. And then the tiny angel reached up, but not for the bell. His hand closed around nothing, yet when he pulled down, light stretched, lengthening into a strand. Insubstantial light became thread, fine as spider's silk, bright as morning.

Taweel was stunned. "I never realized …!"

"You never *noticed*."

He watched the little one work, awed by this new discovery. "I thought all the yahavim did was make manna."

Loris returned to his stitching before quietly stating, "God provides for our needs whether we notice His foresight or not."

31

Now I Lay Me

Taweel gazed up at the busy yahavim, whose strands were steadily taking shape. "Is it a nest?"

Weft frowned in confusion. "What is that?

Something of earth, unknown to this child of heaven. "A place where young ones sleep when they are tired."

"Sleep?"

Taweel folded his hands under his cheek and closed his eyes. "This is how humans enter dreams."

"Humans build nests?" Weft asked.

The warrior patted his cot. "Something like this, soft and safe."

Tapping his fingers on the place Taweel had claimed, the boy asked, "Is this *your* nest?"

Maybe so. He ruefully answered, "For now."

32
FOR GOD

Through the watches, Taweel admired the miniature work of art taking shape under the hands of a yahavim with pale blue hair. "How do you transfer their thread onto your spools?"

Loris smiled. "Carefully."

"Do they mind that you undo their efforts?"

The Weaver paused in his stitching. "Each time the yahavim spin, they create something beautiful for God. A gift. And when He accepts their offering, He gives it a new shape. A purpose." Loris peered up at the tiny angel as he answered the Guardian's actual question. "They *don't* mind. And I admire the simplicity of their trust."

33

Deserving

nother yahavim turned up to claim a wreath. As the little one spun, Taweel found himself envying his patient, peaceful pastime. Suddenly, the tiny angel started and turned to look over his shoulder at Taweel. Faceted eyes widened slightly, then blinked.

Taweel grunted in surprise. It was that yellow-haired one from before.

They stared at one another for some time. Then the yahavim shifted around so his back was to the Guardian.

Snubbed.

Taweel didn't doubt that he deserved the little angel's derision. After all, the sprite was faithfully tending to his duties while his audience wasted away in shadows.

34
Sneak

Taweel felt the yahavim land on his forehead, but he didn't open his eyes. If ignored, the spinners usually wandered off.

This one didn't. Small feet stepped lightly along his nose, and with a fluttering hop, landed on the Guardian's chin. Suddenly, a tiny arm pushed past Taweel's lips, followed by a heady explosion of sweetness in his mouth.

His first taste of manna since his charge's death.

Tears welled in Taweel's eyes, preventing him from seeing which of the yahavim had taken it upon himself to force-feed a dimming warrior.

More amused than annoyed, Taweel grumbled, "Audacious little thing."

35
STARVED

W hen Weft returned, he made a soft noise of dismay and reached up to touch Taweel's tear-streaked face. "What happened?"

"One of your friends fed me."

After a long pause, the boy said, "It wasn't one of *my* flock. I was just tending them."

"A wild one, then?"

"No. Wild yahavim spin thread. Manna is brought by those with a shepherd." Weft cautiously asked, "Were you hungry?"

Taweel grunted noncommittally. He'd been refusing meals, but that single taste of angel's bread had stirred his appetite for more.

Weft explained, "If you're hungry, they know. Yahavim always know when they're needed."

36
COMMISERATION

Every time Taweel closed his eyes, he'd catch the whisper of wings. He never peeked because he had the impression that his benefactor didn't like his task. But once Sent, the tiny angel would have no choice but to obey.

So the next time the little manna-maker landed on his shoulder, Taweel murmured, "Do you miss your spinning?"

The yahavim froze.

"I miss …." Taweel's voice cracked. "I did not wish to abandon my task either."

His visitor hummed uncertainly.

Taweel sighed wearily. "I am sorry, little one. The threads were pretty."

The warrior was ill-prepared for what happened next.

37
TINY PERFECTIONS

Tiny feet marched up Taweel's cheek. Then the yahavim grabbed several eyelashes and yanked open his lid. Taweel grunted in surprise at the miniature person filling his view. Straight hair framed a cherubic face— round cheeks, pointed chin, knit brows. And squeaking. Lots of squeaking.

"Have I offended you, little one?"

An emphatic buzz of wings accompanied chatter that was more emotion than sense. Indignation was plain on a face dominated by large, slanted eyes with rainbow colors glittering across dark facets.

Taweel quietly remarked, "You have pretty eyes."

The little angel stopped mid-squeak … blinked … and let go.

38
GOOD BOY

Weft found them still staring at one another. "You tamed one!" he rejoiced.

The yahavim flipped long yellow hair.

These tiny angels were intuitive and intelligent, but they couldn't speak for themselves. So Taweel corrected the boy. "If he is tame, it is by his choice, not my doing."

Wee eyebrows arched, and the yahavim leapt into the air, turning a tight somersault that condensed light into a translucent flake. Flying into the Guardian's face, the sprite shoved the manna into Taweel's mouth, then patted his cheek as if to say, *good boy*.

"Perhaps this little one is taming me."

39
HE NEEDS A NAME

"What's his name?" asked Weft.

Taweel shook his head. "How would I know?"

"Because he looks to you."

At a loss, the Guardian gruffly said, "He did not mention a name."

Weft giggled, and with the crook of a finger, he coaxed the little angel over. Nonsensical chatter. Gentle praise. Murmured suggestions. One must have pleased the yahavim, for he brightened considerably, then darted into the vines overhead to unwind a length of gleaming thread from his abandoned wreath.

Weft used it to tie his long, yellow hair into a high ponytail before making an introduction. "Taweel, this is Omri."

40
OMRI

Omri rushed at Taweel, who lifted his hands to fend off the tiny attacker. Weft dissolved into giggles, and the Guardian sheepishly lowered his hands. To Taweel's surprise, the little one landed on his knuckles. Up on tiptoe, hands clasped behind his back, he leaned forward … waiting.

"Omri," Taweel said, tasting the name and finding it pleasant. "I am Taweel."

The yahavim sprang upward, capered around the room in a wild aerial dance, finally coming to rest with a flop on Taweel's head.

Holding very still, he asked, "Is this normal behavior?"

Weft nodded eagerly. "Happiness is for sharing!"

Take a Hint

Taweel finally calmed the little angel enough to listen. "I am glad there is peace between us. Now you may go your own way."

The yahavim didn't budge.

"You can go, little one."

Omri tipped his head to one side and blinked.

Taweel firmly repeated, "*Go.*"

With a puzzled expression, he finally took the hint.

Loris leaned into the alcove. "He'll be back."

"He is free to do as he chooses."

"Omri has *chosen* you."

Taweel grumbled, "Have you ever heard of any of my order tending to yahavim?"

"No." With a knowing smile, the Weaver repeated, "He'll be back."

42
Hunger Pangs

Taweel understood what it meant to fight. Against staggering odds. Against princes and principalities. But Omri was a force he didn't know how to combat. The yahavim brought manna at odd intervals to keep him from dimming. Except it was never quite enough. Omri only succeeded in making Taweel crave more of the stuff.

"Do you know what you are doing?" he asked, even though the little one couldn't answer.

With every portion, Omri proved that God's mercy was sweet.

"You have an unfair advantage."

It was the simple truth. Omri *would* win. Because Taweel was counting on his success.

CONSEQUENCES

The next time Weft visited Taweel's hiding place, he brought along a yahavim with a tuft of icy blue hair who shone like a star. While the young Weaver showed off a skein of thread he'd dyed purple, Taweel kept half an eye on the game of chase happening overhead. Something nagged at him until finally, he asked, "Why is that little one so much brighter than Omri?"

Weft answered quietly. "Yahavim *need* light."

"Heaven is awash. The supply is as endless as eternity."

Weft's slender hands indicated the alcove. "But Omri lingers in shadows."

"With me," Taweel whispered, thunderstruck.

44
Double Standard

Taweel found himself in the absurd position of giving advice he refused to take himself.

"You need to leave these shadows. Children of light must dwell in light!"

Omri simply mimicked the Guardian's arms-folded stance.

How could one so small cause such an uproar? The answer was simple. Taweel remembered how a baby's first squall had sent him to his knees. And this was like that. "Please, little one. I love you too much to let you dwindle away."

Then Taweel bowed his head and wept, for it was as if God had spoken the very same words to him.

Taweel stood on his cot and reached up to set Omri in his wreath, where the light was stronger. "Sit there. Stay."

With a moody *meep*, he did. But only long enough for the Guardian to retreat.

Once Taweel stretched out on his cot, Omri dropped, not once fanning his wings to slow his fall. Lurching forward, Taweel caught him. "What was that?" he demanded worriedly.

But Omri simply lay with his cheek pressed to Taweel's palm, limp and listless. Which was more than enough to firm his resolve. Thrusting aside the alcove's curtain, Taweel stepped out into the light.

46
WALK IN THE LIGHT

Loris's home was so unlike the tents of Guardians, which smelled of oil, leather, and polish. Taweel's nose twitched at the mingling of unusual odors. Instead of the *crack* of weapons and rhythmic grind of whetstones found in hadarim encampments, he heard *clack*ing looms and excited chatter. But there was light aplenty, and that was most important.

"Better?" he asked in hushed tones.

Omri spread his hands wide as if welcoming the light's embrace.

Cradling the yahavim close, Taweel closed his eyes and lifted his face to the sky. Little breezes ruffled his hair in gentle greeting. "Better," he sighed.

TRIED AND TRUE

47
BLENDED FAMILY

Taweel followed the sound of trickling water into an enclosed garden. Evidences of Loris's expertise were everywhere—dye pots, thread skeins, heaps of shimmering cloth. The Weaver knelt before a frame, four needles flying as he chatted with his apprentice.

Weft looked enough like his mentor to give the impression that they were father and son. Impossible, but oddly comforting. Taweel had lost his charge, his mentor, his captain. But these two felt like a family.

Loris glanced up. "Join us!"

Weft hurriedly dragged over another cushion, tutting over Omri as Taweel took his new place. A Guardian among Weavers.

48
Ties that Bind

"Does a Weaver ever stop?" Taweel asked.

Loris nudged Weft, who giggled and said, "Only to thread his needle."

A joke. But not far from the truth. The beghedim lived up to their industrious reputation.

"A new Flight has been formed for a young captain," Loris remarked.

Taweel wondered how he stayed so well-informed. "Who told you?"

"Raiment serves more than one purpose. See? It's all here." Sea-green thread gleamed on the collar Loris had been embellishing. "These patterns tell a story. They connect this cherub to his new men, his old mentor, his comrades, his Creator. And to me."

49
BRONZE THREAD

Taweel stared at his tunic sleeve. The absence of embroidery had appealed to him, but he realized something important. "The weave itself still connects me to the maker."

Loris patted the warrior's broad shoulder. "And that's me."

Weft tapped the back of Taweel's hand and asked, "Will you let me add your name?"

"It would be excellent practice." Loris reached without looking and chose the thread used for hadarim. "Provided your burly apprentice doesn't mind being claimed by such a young mentor …?"

Faced by the boy's pleading gaze, Taweel gave in. "Training is essential. I am in your hands."

50
Comfort Zone

"Enough, little one." Taweel caught Omri between strong fingers. "Rest from your manna-making and enjoy the ride."

With a hum, the yahavim fluttered free and settled on the Guardian's bare shoulder.

Since Weft needed more time to finish stitching Taweel's collar, Loris had loaned him a warrior's sleeveless tunic. The small change helped Taweel feel more like himself, which was probably why he was falling back on old habits.

Carefully marking the location of Loris's home, the Guardian entered the street. Even though no danger could befall his new family here, he'd rest easier knowing the lay of the land.

51

ESTABLISHING A PERIMETER

Street by street, Taweel paced off the entire Weavers' district. Since his arrival, he'd blocked out the ebb and flow of life here. Now, he threaded his way through the crowd, watching for patterns, learning their ways.

The beghedim didn't have captains or Flights. They needed no training grounds. But like every district he'd seen during his wandering, there was a central circle. Stone rings provided seating, fanning out from a low pedestal where one of the Worshipers would offer the endless, overlapping songs that marked the watches. Even now, Taweel could hear a voice. And it broke his heart.

52
Heaven's Decorations

Worshipers were made for song, and they often led their angelic brethren in worship. Taweel hadn't planned to go anywhere near the circle. How could he tune his heart to praise when it was heavy with grief? But this Worshiper wasn't in the circle.

He stood in a small garden surrounded by candle-trees, his wings outstretched. The zamarim were sometimes called heaven's decorations, for their wings were exquisite. Beauty and harmony, light and music. This particular Worshiper had deep blue hair feathering away from his forehead like exotic plumage.

And his song was sad enough to pierce Taweel's mournful heart.

53

LOST IN THE CROWD

Taweel wasn't the only angel drawn in by the impromptu song. Loitering on the crowd's fringes with eyes downcast, he listened intently. The Worshiper grieved for the plight of Creation in a way that made Taweel wonder if he'd also mingled with mankind. He reminded God of His promise. He pleaded for a redeemer. He sang of a faith that would become sight.

As the final note faded, Omri chirruped, and Taweel glanced up … meeting the Worshiper's waiting gaze.

With a sleepy smile, the angel nodded a greeting. Or maybe it was goodbye. Because he turned and drifted away.

54
Teach the Curious

Taweel sat next to his little mentor, watching him work. "Are those letters?"

"*No*," Weft giggled.

"But there's meaning to the patterns," Loris clarified. "Teach the curious, child."

So the young Weaver narrated his stitching, unraveling one of heaven's little mysteries. Taweel was impressed enough to ask for more details. Weft cheerfully deciphered the embroidery on his own sleeve, then on Loris's pant-cuff. Row on row, their stories unfolded.

"We'll need to dye more bronze thread," Loris casually remarked. "A Caretaker recently arrived with twelve youngsters."

"New angels?" Weft asked eagerly.

"So new, they still have stardust between their toes!"

55
CIRCUIT

No day. No night. But work and worship lent an orderly pattern to eternity, as natural as breathing. Taweel watched over the comings and goings in the Weavers' district like a one-warrior Hedge. Well … if you counted Omri, *two* angels made a regular circuit.

"I could not read embroidery until I asked a Weaver," Taweel murmured to his little passenger. "Who can teach me the patterns of the Worshipers' rotation?"

Omri hummed along with the red-haired angel on the pedestal. His tenor rose sweetly to the sky, but Taweel turned away, dissatisfied.

Where was the Worshiper with blue hair?

56
If I Had Wings

"Help me reach the wreaths?" Weft pointed into the branches of the candle-tree that arched over their fountain.

Taweel knelt, asking, "How did you hang them in the first place?"

"A ladder. But if I had wings, I'd fly up." The boy came closer, but didn't climb on. "*You* have wings."

"You know I do."

Fingers lightly brushed the purple patterns on the warrior's dusky skin. "May I see?"

Weft had indulged Taweel's curiosity about Weavers often enough. "How close have you been to an angel unfurled?"

"Not very." he daringly added, "Until now …?"

Taweel's lips quirked. "Step back."

Unfurled

He prolonged the display for Weft's benefit. Leafy patterns shifted. Light slowly lifted away from Taweel's broad shoulders and the backs of his arms. Translucent layers of purple swirled outward.

Weft gasped in delight and mimicked the Guardian's wingspan. "May I see?" he begged.

"Your eyes are open."

The young Weaver wiggled his fingers, and Taweel grunted. Beckoning the boy closer, he enfolded him in swaths of light. To his amusement, Weft gathered the stuff close and rubbed it against his cheek.

"Fine. Soft," he crooned. Pausing to listen to the music that whispered through Taweel's wings, Weft added, "Sad."

58
LOST POSSIBILITIES

Taweel withdrew to his shadowy alcove. Not to stay. Omri needed light. But the Guardian's mood had taken a downturn. "So young. So innocent."

Omri didn't answer. Only crawled through Taweel's thick hair, humming nonsense.

Having a child wrapped safe in his wings made Taweel remember. And all the lost possibilities tasted like regret and shame. No wonder his wings whispered sadness. Could that sorrow taint Weft? "I should go. For his sake."

He'd nearly talked himself into leaving when a soft scuffle came from Loris's workroom … followed by excited whispers. Escape would have to wait. Taweel was cornered.

59

TEST OF COURAGE

Taweel's heart clenched when the patter of feet approached his hideaway's entrance. A fair hand eased past the curtain, creating a gap. Brown eyes peeped through … and widened. A matching set peered in much closer to the floor, and Taweel sighed. Young warriors liked tests of courage.

Omri spotted their intruders and rushed at them, squeaking furiously.

A yelp. A scramble. A thud. And Weft giggling through it all.

Taweel intoned, "This victory belongs to Omri. May you fare better in your next match."

This time, three boys poked their heads around the corner. Weft and his newfoundling friends.

60
ℐNNOCENTS

As soon as the boys slipped into his lair, Taweel's guard slammed down. Weft's friends wore raiment edged in bronze thread. These hadarim were newer than new, with skinny arms and rounded cheeks. Shy and tongue-tied. Had he ever been that innocent?

Anger and sorrow tangled in Taweel's heart. Those soft hands would soon be callused by training. Those bare feet would soon be shod for war. Those young boys would clap a breastplate over their hearts, but it wouldn't protect them. Because in the fullness of time, like so many other guardian angels before them, they would be pierced.

61
SHOW OFF

Weft clambered up beside the burly warrior, all smiles. "*Told* you I had an apprentice! This is Taweel."

The first newfoundling elbowed his friend. "He's *big*."

"He is like us," murmured the second.

Their matched expressions of awe flustered Taweel, but he could remember being impressed by older, more confident members of his order … *and* craving their acknowledgment. Unable to withhold something as simple as his attention, Taweel extended a hand. "Are you not Guardians? Where is your courage?"

The boys traded grins before accepting his challenge. Rushing into the shadowy alcove, they placed their hands trustingly into his.

62
LOOK ALIKE

The newfound Guardians were head-and-shoulders taller than their friend. Long limbs. Big feet. They jostled each other, testing their inherent strength, but their gentleness with Weft distinguished them as hadarim. Even while goofing off, they hemmed him in. Playing Hedge.

"You look like brothers," Taweel remarked, struck by their obvious similarities.

"What's that?" asked the first boy.

Weft giggled. "Brothers are for men, not angels!"

Taweel explained, "When human boys are born into the same family, they are brothers."

"And two born together are called twins." Leaning through the doorway, Loris cheerfully asked, "Do my young guests have names yet?"

63
ANOTHER NAME

Every angel knew their own name. It was a secret they cherished, a gift from God. But somewhere along the way, newfoundlings were given another name. There was no rhyme or reason to who assigned them or when. Names had a way of happening.

The first boy tapped his chest. "The Messenger who brings our manna called me Adin."

"A handsome name," Loris decreed. "And you?"

The other newfoundling simply shook his head.

Adin linked arms with his friend. "How about … twin?"

Loris hummed thoughtfully. "Tamaes *means* twin. Will that do?"

Weft applauded the choice. "Tamaes is Adin's twin!"

64
TERMS OF AFFECTION

Explanations continued as Loris ushered his young guests into the garden. "Weft is my apprentice, and Taweel is his. What could be simpler?"

Adin pointed out, "He's not a Weaver."

"He is like us," repeated Tamaes.

Weft stubbornly insisted, "Taweel's ours!"

"He's God's," countered Adin.

"We *all* belong to God." Loris kept his tone light, yet firm. "But when friendships take special shapes, they beg for names. We are Taweel's family, just as you boys are brothers. Taweel is as much Weft's apprentice as you are Tamaes's twin. These aren't terms of fact, but affection."

Adin smiled shyly at Taweel. "Belonging's nice."

65
SHIELD

While Weft chatted to his friends about the recent arrival of seasoned Guardians in their district, Taweel wrestled for composure. Omri's croon was the only hint at his inner turmoil, but it caught the second boy's attention. The big warrior stared miserably into Tamaes's reddish-brown eyes. Was training these children to be strong the *only* way to protect them?

Taweel's desire to shelter them from the future took an unexpectedly practical turn. As if by their own accord, his wings unfurled in a magnificent rush.

Both hadarim gasped, and Adin exclaimed, "Teach us how!"

Tamaes nodded just as eagerly. "Please?"

66
COAXING

Weft exclaimed, "You can teach them to fly?"

Taweel scrutinized the other two boys standing in the circle of his wings. Adin and Tamaes shuffled their feet, and Adin said, "Before we can *fly* ...."

Tamaes finished, "... we must learn to unfurl."

"Is it hard to do?" asked Weft.

"No," assured Taweel. "Unfurling only needs a little coaxing. But flight will take lengthy practice."

"How do you coax wings?" asked Weft, who peered closely at Adin's arms. The boy's furled wings lay in bold rings, like bangles of varying widths encircling his upper arms.

Taweel's gaze dropped. "With song."

Songs in the Night

"Training camps observe evensong," Taweel explained. The weapons masters and prospective mentors who oversaw each newfoundling's progress would bring in guest Worshipers to help the young ones along. "Most learn to unfurl then."

"Evensong?" asked Weft.

Adin spoke first. "On earth, when day becomes night, angels gather for worship."

"Children of light sing in darkness," Tamaes added.

"We've had three evensongs," Adin reported. "But no one's figured it out."

Taweel huffed in amusement. "Impatient?"

"Yes!" exclaimed Adin.

Tamaes nodded. "We were made to fly!"

Taweel asked, "Do you sing for wings, or for the One who gave them to you?"

68
EVASIVE MANEUVERS

"Does it have to be a Worshiper?" asked Weft.

Taweel reluctantly admitted, "No."

"Does it have to happen during evensong?"

"No."

Adin and Tamaes traded excited glances. "Here? Now?"

Taweel gruffly replied, "Wait for your masters and mentors to guide you. They would want to share …."

"Sing with us!" Adin begged.

Tamaes worked hard to catch the big warrior's gaze. "Please?"

Hastily furling his wings, Taweel stood. "I need to check the perimeter."

He didn't even make it to the door.

Adin slipped his hand into Taweel's. "We'll help!"

Tamaes's fingers tangled with his. "We will join your Hedge."

ONE OF A KIND

Differences in the boys' appearance became increasingly obvious to Taweel. While both had brown eyes, Adin's were clear as topaz, but Tamaes's had a reddish cast, like mahogany. And Adin's hair was a slightly darker shade of auburn.

Tamaes peered up in a puzzled way. "I think that yahavim followed us. Is he lost?"

"No. This is Omri."

"He *attacked* us before," Adin said, sounding impressed.

Tamaes's eyes crossed when Omri zoomed in close and tapped his nose. "Is he yours?"

Taweel's grunt and Omri's squeak came at the same time, making it tricky to tell who belonged to whom.

70
HIM

Taweel missed having a child under his watch-care, but these boys would soon be paired off with mentors. Getting attached would be foolish. Jaw set. Eyes averted. Guard up. He escorted Adin and Tamaes toward the hadarim encampment.

"Listen!" whispered Tamaes, stopping in the middle of the street.

"It's him!" Adin tugged Taweel's hand. "This way!"

His feet dragged, but the boys pushed and pulled him along. A confident song, rich with emotion, rose from the circle. When its singer held out his hands, Adin and Tamaes darted forward, abandoning Taweel, who stood anchored.

It *was* him. The blue-haired angel.

71
WRONG

At a whispered word from the Worshiper, the boys rushed back to Taweel, preventing his escape.

"Asaph is nice," Tamaes promised, leading him toward the seated angel.

"He led our first evensong," Adin explained before switching his attention to Asaph. "Can you help? Taweel thinks we sang wrong before, because we sang for ourselves. But he *doesn't* sing, so he can't help us unfurl."

Tamaes squeezed Taweel's hand. "Weft told us."

"An angel without a song?" Wide-set green eyes noted the amateurish stitching at Taweel's collar, the yahavim perched on his head, and his pierced ear. "Yes, I can help."

72
I Can Help

Taweel shrank from the offer Asaph's words held. Hadn't God made him to love his charge? Was he wrong to grieve?

But the Worshiper made no demands. Focusing on Adin and Tamaes, Asaph asked, "Will you sing with me?"

Words and melody. Worship and harmony. He led them in a song of faithful service, trust in their Creator, and hope for a joy that would be full.

Face blank. Tongue locked. Eyes dry. Taweel still couldn't bring himself to sing, even when the sweet duet of praise brought a telltale sparkle to the wings furled against the boys' slender arms.

Blooming Colors

Even the boys' furled wings were similar—both in shades of orange. Adin's bold bangles encircled his upper arms. Tamaes's were decorated by a profusion of delicate rings that began to separate from his skin, edges fluttering.

Adin unfurled first, revealing wings the hue of ripe musk melons, faintly blushed with rose. They quivered in limp folds as he drew them around his friend. Tears streaked his upturned face as their duet continued.

Tamaes's wings emerged in a broader range of colors, from deep oranges to gleaming amber. The blend reminded Taweel of firelight.

Both were beautiful—flower and flame.

74
EVERMORE

The expectancy in Asaph's gaze reminded Taweel that as the only other Guardian present, his words were needed. Kneeling, he grasped the boys' shoulders and declared, "Adin and Tamaes have found their wings."

Adin managed a crooked flap. "Yes!"

"May they shelter those you love," Taweel continued.

Scrubbing tears from his cheeks, Tamaes mumbled, "Someone to love."

Taweel finished by quoting the same words Dorum had used to welcome him as a fully-fledged hadarim. "God gave you life; live for Him. He gave you strength; learn its limits. He gave you songs; sing evermore."

Asaph smiled serenely. "Amen and amen."

Eager to tell Weft about their accomplishment, the boys ran off, leaving Taweel with Asaph. Folding his hands together, the blue-haired angel inquired, "Do you want to ask me anything?"

"No."

He accepted that with a nod, but predicted, "That will change."

Taweel grunted, but he couldn't deny it. There was something about this Worshiper that tugged at his aching heart.

"May I share a song?"

Taweel's head hung low as a melancholy melody filled the space between them. Heavy with sadness. Tangled with unanswerable questions. Lashed with frustration and confusion. The song was Asaph's, but its cry was Taweel's.

76
Yes and No

Feet scuffed, and Taweel's gaze slanted toward the courtyard entrance where two boys in need of lessons in stealth stood gawking at him. Questioning the wisdom of whatever Guardian oversaw the hadarim encampment, he asked, "Do your teachers know you wandered away?"

Adin nodded. Tamaes shook his head.

"We have permission," Adin clarified. "But we're not wandering."

"You told your teachers about me?" Taweel shuddered to think what they thought of a prodigal warrior who played at Hedge.

Tamaes nodded. Adin shook his head.

They elbowed each other, and Tamaes explained, "We told them we share a secret with God."

Consider Your Ways

"A secret … with God?"

"Yes!" Adin exclaimed, eyes shining. "We didn't unfurl our wings first, but we're the first to be Sent!"

Taweel slowly shook his head, echoing, "*Sent*?"

"To you," Tamaes confirmed.

"But *why*?"

The boys traded looks, then shrugged. Adin said, "God didn't say. Does it matter?"

He shook his head yet again. "You did well to obey. When an angel is Sent, he goes."

Adin struck a pose. "And here we are!"

"Because we are Faithful," agreed Tamaes. "Like you."

Taweel was suddenly faced by a sobering thought. These boys wanted to be like him.

78
SHARE AND SHARE ALIKE

While Adin talked, Tamaes eased closer to Taweel and shyly touched his arm. The warrior's muscles were *huge*. Would he and Adin ever be as strong?

Taweel grunted, and Tamaes glanced up. He'd been caught.

"Question?" the warrior invited in a gruff undertone.

Tamaes froze under the weight of his solemn gaze, but Omri dove off Taweel's shoulder and landed on Tamaes's nose. Eyes crossing, the boy whispered, "Only *one*?"

When he refocused on the warrior's face, Taweel's expression had softened. Tamaes wished he knew if the gentle look was for Omri or for him. But he didn't mind sharing.

CALLED INTO QUESTION

Until Adin and Tamaes started dropping by at regular intervals, Taweel hadn't appreciated Weft's capacity for tact.

"Why are you barefoot?" asked Adin.

Taweel pointed out, "Your feet are also bare."

"Only because our feet are still too small."

Tamaes asked, "What weapons did you learn?"

Before Taweel could answer, Adin started pushing at his sleeves. "Why is your tunic different from other Guardians? Can I see your furled wings?"

Taweel flinched when fingers brushed his earring.

"Oh," breathed Tamaes, his wide eyes begging for forgiveness. "Does it still hurt?"

A quick headshake. A small nod. "It does," Taweel confessed.

80
ROGUE GUARDIAN

Hadarim were arriving from every district and quarter. Experienced warriors. Patient teachers. Prospective mentors.

Valerian's conversation with the encampment's overseer trailed off when two cherubim arrived. Without preamble the first announced, "We have news about the rogue Guardian."

"Our mysterious recluse!" To Valerian, the overseer explained, "He cast aside armor and armaments and dresses in the manner of Weavers. Adin and Tamaes think him *wonderful*."

"You are concerned for the boys' safety?" Valerian asked.

"No. But what's changed?"

The cherub reported, "Someone added stitching to his collar. An apprentice's work, but legible."

"What does it say?"

"Only a name. Taweel."

"Glide. Arrow. Slow. Pivot. Rise." Tamaes struggled through wing positions, then sighed, "This is *hard*."

"Flight takes strength," Taweel replied. "You need more."

The boy glanced up at his twin, who was scrambling through the candle-tree with Weft. "Adin makes it look easy."

"We each earn our own piece of sky."

Resuming his exercises, Tamaes lost contact with the ground when a breeze caught his *rise* position.

Taweel casually snagged the boy's ankle, mooring him. "Again," he coached. "Rise."

Tamaes's next wingbeat caught more air, and Taweel grunted approvingly. No harm in giving the boy a tiny taste of flight.

82
Testing His Wings

Tamaes yearned to test his wings, but the teachers in the hadarim encampment told them over and again: feet on the ground. Training exercises were tedious, and all the newfoundlings were restless for the next things—boots, armor, weapons. But *especially* flight.

"Again. Rise," urged Taweel.

Was it all right? This Guardian wasn't one of his teachers, but Tamaes didn't think Taweel would lead him astray. A strong hand. A faint smile. Encouragement. Permission.

'He offers a good gift.'

Taking God at His word, Tamaes flexed his wings. Safely anchored by the big warrior, he threw himself at the sky.

Reap the Whirlwind

Tamaes's efforts resembled the frantic fluttering of a sparrow caught in a snare. Taweel ordered, "Straighten your shoulders. Relax your knees."

With a sheepish glance, the boy corrected his form.

"Slow your pace. Faster is not always better."

"Like this?" Tamaes asked, settling into a steadier rhythm.

Taweel grunted. "Your training serves you well."

Their partnership didn't go unnoticed. From his perch overhead, Adin exclaimed, "Me, too!"

"I have two hands."

While the boys stirred a whirlwind, Taweel felt a tug at his earring. Omri squeaked in apology, but he didn't let go. The little angel desperately needed his handhold.

84
MAKING DO

"Only hadarim form Hedges," Adin said. "That leaves out Weft."

"So we will be a Flight," explained Tamaes.

Taweel grunted. "Traditionally, cherubim serve as Flight captains."

Adin frowned. "We don't have a cherub."

"And Flights have twelve angels." Taweel wondered what Dorum would say if he knew his former apprentice dressed like a Weaver and played at Flight and Hedge with newfoundlings.

"Easy!" Weft exclaimed.

The boys soon dubbed Taweel the first-ever Guardian captain, and Weft painted their names on his palm, including Loris, Omri, and the five yahavim in Weft's flock.

"That's eleven," Adin reported. "We need one more."

ONE MORE

Adin jumped up. "I'll go find someone!"

"Is that how it works?" Tamaes asked. "Maybe God will Send someone."

Weft's dozen toes wriggled. "I don't know. This isn't a *proper* Flight."

"We're training," argued Adin.

Tamaes softly said, "We are playing."

"*And* learning," Weft reminded. "Taweel is teaching us."

The boys traded uncertain glances, and Taweel's heart ached. Even if this was only a boys' game, they'd placed their names in his hand. He lightly touched the crooked rows of letters on his palm and wondered what God was doing.

Just then, a voice came from out front. "Anyone home?"

86
TWELFTH

Loris escorted his unexpected guest into the garden. "You have God's own timing. The boys were hoping for a twelfth."

"Rather call me God's own provision, for I was Sent." Asaph extended his hands to the trio of young ones. "You have need of a Worshiper?"

The boys excitedly outlined their plans, tugging at Asaph's sleeves until he knelt beside the Guardian sitting in the corner.

"Taweel's our leader!" Adin exclaimed.

Tamaes added, "Weft put our names on his hand!"

"I shall trust myself to Taweel's keeping." With a sleepy smile, Asaph inquired, "Will you trust yourself to mine, Captain?"

Step in the Right Direction

Training exercises turned into a game of chase through a grove of candle-trees, with three excitable boys in pursuit of their Flight's half-dozen yahavim members. They disbanded after a final song, and Taweel found himself alone with Omri … and Asaph.

Without a word, the blue-haired Worshiper drifted off, out of step with the Weaver district's busyness. Taweel only hesitated for a few moments before trailing after him.

Asaph glanced over his shoulder and asked, "Are you ready?"

Taweel's steps faltered. "For what?"

The Worshiper backtracked to place his hand over the Guardian's broken heart. "Are you ready to sing?"

88
Not Alone

Asaph slowly reached up and touched Taweel's left ear.

The Guardian knew he had no reason to be ashamed of the heavy silver ring that pierced his lobe. Most hadarim who'd served in Time were pierced, for the world had Fallen. Still, he flinched.

"Is the grief still so fresh?" asked the Worshiper.

Taweel lowered his gaze. Self-conscious. Ashamed. Every guardian angel held out hope that their charge would come to faith. He wasn't alone in his disappointment.

"You did all you could," Asaph said gently. "For the one you refuse to forget."

Taweel's jaw tightened. "It was not enough."

Precious in His Sight

"You and I were never *meant* to be enough," Asaph gently reminded.

"I know it," Taweel gruffly replied. "But she was mine to watch over. Mine to love as God loves."

"Yes," the Worshiper agreed. "I am no Guardian, but I have witnessed the songs of many hadarim. Members of your order are faithful to love each and every life. But not all who are loved respond to the One who counts them precious."

"Mine never knew."

Asaph nodded. "And so your heart broke."

Taweel's voice shook. "That is how it feels."

"Naturally," Asaph murmured. "Because God's heart also breaks."

90
WALK BY FAITH

Asaph spoke calmly of things Taweel already knew. "Angels begin their lives as Faithful, but some do Fall. Humans begin as Fallen, but some do have faith. And each time a Guardian's charge chooses to live by faith …?"

"There is fullness of joy," Taweel finished in roughened tones.

"And the source of our joy and rejoicing?"

"God, who made us all."

Nodding, Asaph prompted, "And how do we express our gratitude for joy?"

"Song."

"Yes," the Worshiper said, his tones gentling further. "And you are neither faithless, nor ungrateful. That is why, my Captain, you *must* find your voice."

Bear Witness

Asaph took his arm. "Come with me to a place apart, and I will bear witness to your song."

Taweel shook his head. "I am unable …."

"Fear not," the Worshiper soothed. "Once we unfetter your voice, you can unburden your heart. Let me lead you into song."

"Where?" he whispered.

"A way has been made." Asaph drew him toward the pavilion at the district's edge, and the area within its ring of stones shimmered. With a crooked smile, the Worshiper lifted his arms. "Lend me your wings?"

Purple light unfurled, and picking up Asaph, Taweel leapt from heaven's threshold.

92
A Place Apart

The way opened, and Taweel expertly banked into a wide turn over a seemingly endless meadow of golden flowers. When the Guardian's bare feet touched the ground, his wings sent a swirl of pollen into the air.

He set Asaph down, and the Worshiper began, "Your heart cries to Me throughout the watches, and I will answer. Meet with Me here, children of light. Let there be peace between us once more."

Taweel dropped to his knees amidst the flowers and murmured his agreement. "My heart does cry."

Asaph sang freely of sorrows, which coaxed Taweel into voicing his complaint.

GOOD GIFT

Hurt and anger. Confusion and apology. Taweel felt like a failure, but his task had been impossible. He'd loved his charge, but his hopes for her hadn't been enough. And more than anything … why was *he* the only one struggling? Was his faith too small?

In the golden meadow with honeybees, Asaph, and Omri bearing witness, Taweel found his voice and bared his soul.

And God answered.

The ragged solo became a duet as Taweel's Maker called him by his secret name. Confident assurances. Gentle reassurances. All leading to the gift of hope in the form of a promise.

94
FOUND OUT

"Can I help?" Taweel asked.

Loris laughed. "I'm afraid you lack the necessary delicacy."

Although perfect for gripping the hilt of a sword, Taweel's hands were too large for the fine threads Weft collected. Still, Loris took pity on the restless Guardian. Which is why Taweel was bent over a row of pots when unexpected guests arrived.

"So it *was* you," said a familiar voice. "The rogue."

Taweel started guiltily.

"I did not expect to find you muddling dye like a Weaver's apprentice."

Scrambling to his feet, Taweel shuffled backward and, after an awkward interval, greeted his former mentor. "Dorum."

Valerian the Overseer

"**V**alerian heard a rumor in the encampment and called for me." Stepping closer, Dorum added, "I am glad he did."

Taweel glanced at the other Guardian, a lean spearman with straw-colored hair gathered into a loose braid. "Overseer," he greeted.

"Yes and no. I'm no longer leader of the encampment where you trained. God Sent me here." After a thoughtful pause, Valerian added, "Adin and Tamaes are under my watch-care."

"They will surely prosper." Taweel hesitantly asked, "Are you also a prospective?"

"We both are," Dorum confirmed.

Taweel understood then. Valerian and Dorum were going to take away the boys.

96
Coming Changes

"Your voice is low," Adin said, hanging onto Taweel's arm.

"Deep," agreed Weft.

"And big," Adin added. "Will my voice get bigger?"

"Your voices will change," Taweel confirmed, unfurling his wings in order to catch Tamaes, who was shyer about demanding attention. The Guardian held all three close while he could. Adin and Tamaes would go to mentors soon, and that would be goodbye. "Many things will change."

"You changed," Tamaes said.

Weft nodded eagerly. "You *sing*!"

"And your wings, too," murmured Tamaes, who was swathed in their purple light.

To Taweel's embarrassment, the boys held their breath and listened.

An angel's wings whispered about the state of his heart. For too long, Taweel's had keened like a winter wind through ice-brittle branches. But the lament had ebbed to faint sighs.

"Better," Adin pronounced.

Weft rubbed the draped folds against his cheek. "But still sad. Are you sad, Taweel?"

"Yes."

"No," Tamaes said at the same time.

When the boy tucked his chin to his chest, Taweel tapped the top of his head. "Feelings overlap and contradict. We could both be correct. What did *you* hear, Tamaes?"

"Loneliness." The young Guardian shyly caught Taweel's full sleeve. "Why are you lonely?"

98
LEARNING THE HARD WAY

"How can I be lonely?" Taweel murmured. "You are here."

Tamaes wasn't satisfied, but he'd learned something new. Asking didn't always bring answers. So he wondered his way through training.

Crack!

Tamaes yelped and dropped his staff.

Adin let his own practice weapon fall. "Why didn't you block?"

"Sorry," he mumbled, awkwardly cradling his hand. Bright droplets slipped between his fingers and spattered the floor.

Taweel called, "Loris, bring bandages!"

"It hurts."

"I know," sighed Taweel. "Try to bear it."

Blinking back tears, Tamaes asked, "Like you?"

"You can do better than me," he gruffly retorted.

Tamaes sincerely doubted it.

TRIED AND TRUE

Leaving Openings

"I'm no Caretaker, but this should do," Loris said, tying off the bandage. "It's not like you to leave openings, Tamaes. Where were your thoughts?"

"Wandering." The boy flexed his fingers and winced. "Wondering."

"About …?"

"Taweel." Glancing at the warrior who coached Adin, Tamaes asked, "Is loneliness a kind of pain?"

"I suppose so."

Tamaes scooted closer to the Weaver. "But we are here."

"I believe Taweel's thoughts are also wandering." Loris wrapped his arm around the boy's shoulders. "Newfoundlings who have found their wings soon find themselves in a mentor's keeping. Taweel is grieving a loss that's coming."

100
ASK

Taweel retreated to his shadowy alcove for a private conversation with Omri. Spreading his hands wide, he said, "See for yourself. I am no longer dim."

With a flit of wings, the yahavim landed on his palm and tiptoed across the names painted there.

"My voice has returned. There are songs I can sing." Taweel pointed out, "You are free to go."

Omri sat.

He amended, "Naturally, you are free to stay."

The little angel responded with a tirade of bossy squeaks.

Taweel cut him off by pulling him close and gruffly begging, "Please, stay."

Omri's sweet chirrup settled matters.

Tamaes's hand hurt, so the weapons master told him to go rest. Partway to the tents, the boy received a Sending. He chased the bright certainty all the way to Weft's home and listened breathlessly to the young Weaver's sing-song recitation in the garden. But a final nudge put Tamaes outside Taweel's dim alcove.

Through the curtain, he could see the Guardian slouched against the wall with Omri sprawled on his chest. Taweel's expression was peaceful. He was humming. Not sad. Not lonely.

"He does not need me," Tamaes whispered, very much confused.

The answer came kindly. *'You need him.'*

102
OFFERING SHELTER

"Tamaes?"

"I am here."

"I can see that." Taweel beckoned. "Show me your hand. Have you been using your wings?"

"My exercises?"

"Wings offer shelter for healing. Move over, Omri." Taweel unfurled his wings, then hauled Tamaes under them.

Wriggling into a comfortable position, he asked, "Wings heal?"

"I am surprised no one told you. Rest here awhile."

Tamaes pressed his ear to Taweel's broad chest. Was his heart broken? Was it lonely? On impulse, he unfurled his own wings, clumsily draping them over Taweel and Omri.

"Yours will work, but a friend's are better," Taweel lectured.

Tamaes smiled. "Good."

No Fault, No Blame

"Where is Adin?"

Tamaes flexed his injured hand. "They began with swords today."

Taweel grunted. "Missing out?"

"Yes." After a thoughtful pause, he added, "And no. I was Sent."

"To me?"

Tamaes nodded.

"Why?"

The boy shrugged.

With another grunt, Taweel said, "We could have our own lesson."

Looking up, Tamaes asked, "Is it my fault you are lonely?"

The Guardian's eyes widened. "Apprentices usually ask when they can have boots and a breastplate."

"You told Adin before. I know those answers."

Taweel sighed. "Guardians wait, meet, and part more than most. Try to be grateful, Tamaes. Regrets are unkind."

104
MEET, PART, WAIT

Swords. Taweel remembered his excitement over finally holding one. They were the weapon of choice for most hadarim, which was probably why they were left to last. If the newfoundlings were testing swords, their selection was imminent.

This meeting would soon end in parting, and Taweel couldn't be grateful. But maybe he could help Tamaes. Give the boy a good memory. A parting gift.

Making up his mind, Taweel announced, "I want to stretch my wings."

"Oh." Tamaes's flame-hued wings trembled, and he tried to retreat.

"Wait." Tightening his embrace, Taweel gruffly asked, "Do you want to come with me?"

105
SEIZE THE SKY

"**I** cannot fly well."

Setting Tamaes down, Taweel promised, "I will not let you fall."

He still hesitated. "Loris said that once a newfoundling finds his wings, he is given to a mentor."

"True."

"If you teach me to fly, I will be Sent away sooner," Tamaes reasoned.

"True," Taweel repeated.

Scuffing the floor with his toe, the boy said, "Maybe we should wait."

The big Guardian crouched. "We were made to fly. Your wings must be restless."

"Yes," Tamaes whispered.

Taweel gruffly declared, "I would *never* withhold this joy from you. Much better to share it while we can."

106
Aerobatics

With strong wingbeats, Taweel carried Tamaes aloft, where they encountered a group of malakim. Young Messengers were in the midst of their own training exercises.

Before Taweel could veer around them, Tamaes blurted, "Are they also newfoundlings?"

One of the Messengers wheeled. All smiles, he cheerfully shared, "We have seven youngsters up here with us. They're getting a feel for wind under their wings."

Taweel expertly caught the breezes he needed to hold his position. "Our goal is similar."

Offering both hands, the Messenger invited, "Why don't you join us? We'd be glad to teach you a trick or two!"

MIXING WITH MESSENGERS

All of Taweel's lessons in flying had focused on the need to build strength, to fly in formation, and to confront enemies in midair. Teamwork was paramount. Battle was inevitable.

Not so for malakim.

Messengers weren't warriors, so their priorities were vastly different. Speed. Maneuverability. And *fun*.

"Watch me!" Tamaes called.

From where he waited with those acting as spotters, Taweel lifted his hand. "His confidence grows," he remarked as Tamaes tucked and rolled.

"And his daring!" agreed their host.

The looping, spinning boy was no longer worried about how *well* he could fly. This was joy ... and enjoyment.

108
Heads Up

"Be ready!" warned the Messenger who'd befriended Taweel. "Their lesson's ending."

The Guardian grunted as one by one, the malakim newfoundlings followed their instructor's command and dropped from the sky. Tamaes hesitated longer than the others, but he also furled his wings.

Omri squeaked, and Taweel surged upward, arms ready.

When he pulled the boy snugly into his chest, Tamaes gasped, "Thank you."

"Testing my resolve?"

"Or mine," Tamaes replied with a shaky smile.

"I promised not to let you fall." As he winged homeward, Taweel remarked, "Omri pulled that stunt once."

"Why?"

Taweel finally answered, "Because I needed him."

Temporary Things

Taweel's Flight was assembled. Asaph and Loris chatted in the garden, where Adin and Tamaes did their best to impress them with their sparring. In the airy workshop, Weft trotted back and forth, hanging up the skeins of delicate thread he pulled from the dye pots Taweel was stirring.

Although most of the big Guardian's attention was caught by the series of ringing notes coming from the boys' practice swords, he noticed two things. Weft was quieter than usual, and all the threads coming from the pots were the same color. "Why does Loris need so much bronze thread?"

Weft flinched.

110
℮UT TO THE QUICK

Weft's expression crumpled, and he darted off in the direction of the alcove.

Taweel had been too wrapped up to notice Weft's struggle. And the boy's choice cut deeply. Was *this* the example he'd set? Springing after the boy, Taweel slammed to his knees in front of the cot and gruffly begged, "Do not retreat into shadows."

"They'll be sad to see me sad," Weft explained. "And they *should* be happy. I was when Loris chose me."

Despite his brave words, tears soon dampened the Guardian's shoulder. And Taweel sang softly of eternal things, like the faithfulness of true friends.

WISDOM BORN OF EXPERIENCE

"Come with me," Asaph urged.

Taweel had difficulty meeting the Worshiper's gaze. "Why?"

"Last chances only come once."

With a curt nod, the Guardian fell in step behind the blue-haired angel. One last watch to herald. One last song before selection sent the encampment's newfoundlings in a dozen different directions.

In the circle, Asaph ascended the squat pedestal and spread his wings. Taweel easily picked out Adin and Tamaes from the crowd. Valerian was there. And Dorum stood by.

Taweel's former mentor met his gaze and smiled faintly. Melancholy laced his expression, and for once, Taweel understood. Dorum missed him.

Taweel eased through the crowd. Once his former mentor realized where he was aiming, Dorum met him partway.

"I have been thoughtless," Taweel began.

Dorum's expression softened. "What gave you that idea?"

"I have been … thinking."

With a low chuckle, Dorum gripped his shoulder, chasing Omri from his perch. "Who is this?"

"Omri is my …."

"… Flightmate?" finished Dorum, his eyes sparkling. "Friend of yahavim! Guardian of Weavers! Captain of newfoundlings! Your exploits are legendary."

Taweel groaned. "How did *you* find out?"

"Adin and Tamaes. There are no secrets when your admirers sing your praises at every evensong."

113

ƖNTO THE ƗIGHT

Even in eternity, where neither sun nor moon hold sway, times come. And a moment drew near. Selection.

Anticipation crackled around the newfoundlings as the final note of Asaph's song faded. While the hadarim herded the boys back to the encampment, Taweel turned his back. Last time he'd walked away; this time, he used his wings.

He drove himself higher than he'd ever flown. Awash in pure light, Omri crooned blissfully, and Taweel chuckled. "God is near, and we are welcome."

Not until he coasted into a slow spiral did Taweel catch the sound of voices calling his name.

114
FLOCK

Seven boys careened upward. "Wait for us!"

"We have a message!"

"Remember us?"

Taweel recognized the young malakim who'd welcomed Tamaes into their training session. "Should you be so high?"

"Fear not!"

"Watch what I can do!"

Their escort caught up, and Taweel offered a bewildered greeting. "Am I part of your lesson?"

"Not exactly," the Messenger replied. "This is a Sending. Their first."

"Their excitement is understandable." Taweel huffed in amusement at their capering. "Have they forgotten the message?"

Whistling sharply, the Messenger signaled for descent, then beckoned for Taweel to follow. "This might be easier on solid ground."

Little Messengers, Little Messages

"Focus!" exclaimed the boys' leader. "What messages do you bring?"

In a twinkling, Taweel stood in a circle of newfoundlings. One announced, "This is the place!"

Taweel glanced around the empty courtyard where they'd set down. "For what?"

A second boy said, "A surprise."

More messages came in quick succession.

"A purpose."

"Your future."

"One that has always been waiting."

"It's a good gift."

The seventh boy urged, "Accept it."

Taweel began, "I do not …."

All the boys touched their fingers to their lips, and in the relative hush, a new sound reached Taweel's ears. Metal scraping against stone.

116
FACE THE FUTURE

As the sound came closer, the Messengers scattered, leaving Taweel alone. Or nearly so.

Omri chirruped a wordless question.

Taweel swallowed against the sudden queasiness in his stomach. Whatever was coming, it *wasn't* something he could walk away from. God was pressing him back into service. To flee was to Fall. So he stood firm—despite his failings, in the midst of confusion, unsure of the future.

Then Tamaes struggled into view, dragging a sword that was far too big for his thin arms. The boy took one look at Taweel and sagged to his knees, panting, "It *is* you."

BLACK STONE

Taweel sat down so fast, his descent to the ground probably qualified as a collapse. The sevenfold message reeled through his head while his heart banged around in his chest.

Mentorship?

"Everyone else was Sent to a person." Tamaes blinked several times, then swiped at his cheek with the back of his hand. "But I was Sent to a sword, and then Sent away."

"This is *my* sword." Reclaiming the familiar blade, Taweel studied the black stone newly set into its hilt. Letters cut deeply into its surface, spelling a single word. A name. The name of his new apprentice.

118
But First

Omri yanked Taweel's earring, then buzzed over to Tamaes, whose fragile expression broke the big Guardian's heart. But first, his new apprentice needed correction. "You were not Sent away."

Tamaes's eyes widened, and a tear slipped down his cheek.

Taweel set aside his sword. "You were Sent to me."

There were words he should say. Formalities to observe. Plans to make. But first, Taweel pulled Tamaes into a crushing embrace. If his heart had trembled at the thought of losing the boys, it quaked at the prospect of keeping this one.

"Are you glad?"

Taweel grunted.

Tamaes whispered, "Me, too."

119
GUIDE AND GUARD

As soon as Taweel collected himself, purple wings flared. "Your name is under my hand. Your shelter is beneath my wings. I will be your guide and your guard."

Tamaes nestled closer and murmured, "I will guard a life."

"With all your might."

"I am not very big."

Taweel huffed. "You will grow."

The boy nodded, then cautiously asked, "Will it be hard?"

"Yes."

"Does it hurt?"

There was no denying it. He held his apprentice's gaze. "Sometimes."

"But I will not be alone?"

Taweel shook his head and pledged, "Your call will be my call. Our strength is doubled."

120
Equipment

Taweel slouched against one of the courtyard columns, contemplating his toes. "We will need boots."

Tamaes nodded eagerly. "Apprentices have boots."

Training was best done in the hadarim encampment, where there were weapons and sparring partners aplenty. But Taweel made no move to leave the peaceful courtyard. Eventually, he remarked, "We also need armor."

"Will I meet the Forgers?"

"Soon." Taweel thought to ask, "What about Adin?"

"He will remain at the encampment." The boy cautiously asked, "Can we …?"

With a small sigh, Taweel said, "I will speak to the overseer."

"That is good. Because Valerian is Adin's mentor."

MENTOR AND APPRENTICE

The loss of a child had driven Taweel into solitude; now a child was leading him back into the throng. But was he ready? The big warrior slowed to a stop and cleared his throat.

Tamaes gazed up at him, all awe and anticipation.

"Before I rejoin the hadarim …."

"*We*," the boy corrected.

Taweel grunted, then began anew. "Before we return to the encampment, I should speak to my mentor."

His apprentice blinked, then brightened. "Weft?"

"Loris has long been my host. His home is my home."

Slipping his hand into Taweel's, Tamaes asked, "And mine?"

"We go together."

122
God's Timing

"You came!" Raising his voice even higher, Weft called, "They're here!"

"And in God's own timing," Loris replied, strolling into the room. "The final stitch has been knotted."

Tamaes hooked Weft's arm and pulled him closer. Tapping the bared blade in Taweel's grasp, he proudly announced, "See the stone? Taweel is my mentor. My name is under his hand!"

Weft giggled. "I *know*! God is wise!"

"How did you know?" Taweel asked, glancing at Loris.

The Weaver smiled broadly. "Your raiment has been prepared, and basins await. Come and wash, and my apprentice and I will see you properly arrayed."

CONFIDENCE BOOST

Steam wisped away from basins of scented water. Not the same as a full bath, but welcome nonetheless. "Do you need assistance?" asked Taweel, whose wings curtained them off from the garden.

Tamaes flushed. "Adin usually helps me."

"At your request?"

"Because I am slow."

Taweel knelt and splashed his face, running his fingers through his hair. "I am in no hurry."

Tamaes plunked down before his basin and began tending his wings with painstaking care.

Hiding the barest of smiles, Taweel set a pace that would allow the boy to learn from his example … and to finish first.

124
ROW UPON ROW

When the Weaver brought out his gift, Tamaes gasped, "New tunics?"

"Full sets for mentor and apprentice," Loris confirmed. "Their workmanship has been one of my greatest joys."

"I helped!" Weft interjected.

Bronze threads gleamed richly against the soft luster of heavenly raiment. Taweel hand trembled as he touched Loris's delicate embroidery. Row upon row, the stitches told his story. Finding and naming. His apprenticeship to Dorum. His mastery of sky and sword. Flight assignments. His calling. Piercing. Wandering. And then Weft's mentoring. Omri's companionship. And Tamaes.

"Will you accept it?" Loris asked.

Taweel bowed his head. "All of it."

DANGEROUS DANCE

Omri was playing a convoluted game of peek-a-boo with Weft from behind Tamaes's damp hair, but the young Guardian only had eyes for his mentor.

Taweel was reacquainting himself with his sword. The blade swished and sang as he slashed through the air, thrusting and pivoting. There was a grim set to the warrior's mouth, but Tamaes could see the joy in this dangerous dance.

Stopping short, Taweel tested the sword's edge with his thumb. His soft grunt sounded displeased, and he glanced up, meeting his apprentice's gaze. "My sword needs a better edge. You wanted to meet the Forgers?"

126
NOT OF HEAVEN

"Do they have a district? Or an encampment?" asked Tamaes, who had to skip every few steps to keep up.

"War and weapons are not of heaven," Taweel explained. "The Forgers dwell in Time."

The boy skidded to a standstill. "We are going into Time?"

"Yes."

"Just us?" Tamaes checked.

"You are no longer bound to the encampment. Your courses are mine to direct."

Tamaes was so happy, his throat ached from holding back a song.

Taweel lowered his voice. "Unless you are … unready?"

Tripping over his own feet in his eagerness, Tamaes exclaimed, "We are going into Time!"

IN THE DARKNESS

Tamaes didn't understand why his mentor insisted on carrying him … until they dropped into darkness. The boy's arms quickly clamped down around his mentor's neck. Braving a shadowed alcove was nothing compared to facing his first night.

Taweel murmured, "Fear not."

From his precarious perch on the warrior's shoulder, Omri squeaked and held out his hand. Tamaes rescued the little angel, cradling him close to his chest while Taweel carried them far from home.

All the while, his mentor explained, "Galaxies are smelts for heaven's Forgers." He spiraled into a nebula-wreathed star cluster. "Their order sings with the constellations."

128
Armorers of Heaven

aweel's bare feet touched gold, which paved a gracefully curving arc suspended like a yahavim's nesting hoop in space.

"It is a circle," Tamaes whispered, tipping his head back so far, he lost his balance.

"Yes, and there are others. Circles within circles."

Despite the surrounding darkness, the ring sparkled like chrysolite. And at its center, veiled in flashing eddies of red and violet, a ball of white-hot light burned.

Tamaes squinted. "Is that a star?"

"It is."

From amidst the blaze emerged a figure who glowed like molten bronze. Four wings. Hoofed feet. And a sword in his hand.

A Heavenly Guard

Tamaes whispered, "Is he a Forger?"

"No. The Fourfold are like us." Taweel offered his sword on upraised palms. "Guardians, but not of humanity."

The boy couldn't take his eyes from the oncoming angel's leonine face. "What do they protect?"

"Many things," replied the Fourfold in a deep, echoing voice. "Stars and seasons. Doors and dreams. Thrones and dominions. Powers and principalities."

Awe shivered up and down Tamaes's spine.

The angel accepted Taweel's blade, then crouched before Tamaes. "Fear not, apprentice. My brothers and I are here to serve you."

With a tentative smile, Tamaes shared, "I have a brother."

130
FOURFOLD

"Breastplates for both, and measure …"

" … their feet. Lacing boots is a challenge. Can he …"

" … learn before leaving?"

"Most do not."

Nodding in unison, the Fourfold chorused, "They do not."

Tamaes liked these new angels, but he found their habit of finishing each other's sentences confusing. What's more, each member of this angelic brotherhood had four names. And four faces. The boy couldn't keep them straight.

Taweel asked, "May I introduce Tamaes to the opanim?"

The Fourfold whose name *might* have been Lapis Innis Merriel Nock answered, "The wheels are turning. Bring your apprentice forward."

Wheels Within Wheels

"Ever-turning. Shining. Burning," recited their guide. "They will take your measure."

"I will go first," offered Taweel, who hoped Tamaes would share his awe for the opanim.

Tamaes's face was a picture of confusion. "Those rings are alive?"

"See for yourself," urged the Fourfold.

The boy tiptoed closer, and the intricate gyrations slowed to a standstill. Catching sight of the living gems set into the rings' inner rims, Tamaes gasped, "He has eyes!"

Taweel stepped to his side and addressed the Forger. "I found my way back, bringing this boy."

"*And* Omri." Tamaes touched the outermost rim and whispered, "Hello."

132
Mark of a Mentor

aweel could no longer see Tamaes. Sentient rings sang as they spun, encompassing the boy in light. But then, his apprentice fearlessly joined the Forger's song with a sweet burst of grateful praise. Good. When Taweel grunted, Omri tugged at his new handhold.

"Do you like your gift?"

The little angel chirruped.

Not only had the opanim shaped the new ear cuff that marked Taweel a mentor, he'd formed the delicate chain that linked it to the ring piercing the Guardian's ear. Omri had been swinging from it ever since its discovery.

Taweel's lips quirked. "All makers delight in details."

133
Finishing Touch

Tamaes's excitement over his new armor redoubled as Taweel worked the straps into place, then added a finishing touch. "Do all Guardians do this?" the boy asked.

"Who can say?"

"Did your mentor do this?" Tamaes pressed.

"Yes. Every time."

"More than once?"

Taweel huffed softly. "I grew."

Realization dawned. "We will be back?"

"Many times." Brushing aside stray flecks, he offered the slim dagger. "Now you."

Tamaes's tongue peeped out of the corner of his mouth as he slowly scratched his name inside Taweel's new breastplate. He liked knowing the inscription would always be there, over his mentor's heart.

134
SHOD FOR WAR

Lost in memories, Taweel hummed the cadences of a battle song as he wove crisscrossing straps around his calves.

"Wait!"

With a blink, he recalled his young companion.

Tamaes sat in a hopeless tangle of bootstraps. "Slower?" he begged.

"Fear not. You will learn." Tying off a final knot, Taweel knelt before his apprentice and gently switched the boy's boots, which were stuck on the wrong feet.

"Oh." Tamaes blushed. "That is better."

Evening up the straps, Taweel casually remarked, "If you practice with Weft, you will soon master the patterns. Until then, this is my service."

Tamaes whispered, "Thanks."

Pushing Limits

Tamaes couldn't ever remember feeling clumsy. When he was newly made, he'd skipped after his Maker without a thought to his feet. But boots were heavy. Scuff and clunk. Tromp and trip. Why had something so simple become such a chore?

When the boy dragged to a stop, Taweel turned. "A little further."

Frustrated tears sprang to Tamaes's eyes. "They are uncomfortable."

Taweel didn't scold. He only repeated, "A little further."

"I will try."

His mentor grunted approvingly, which helped a little. But then Taweel offered his hand. That was even better. Holding tight, Tamaes found enough grit to persevere.

136
SELECTIVE HEARING

Walking and talking. It reminded Tamaes of his beginning, when God took him by the hand and taught him what it meant to love and be loved. Now, he needed to learn how to guard one precious life. Then he could love as he was loved.

Taweel squeezed his hand. "Are you listening?"

"Sorry," Tamaes mumbled. "Say it again?"

With a quizzical look, his mentor returned to his rambling lecture. "Raiment and manna are supplied by heaven. They were and are and will be. But armor and weapons are part of creation. They will pass away."

Tamaes's heart leapt. "Weapon?"

"The opanim do not forge weapons for the untested," Taweel cautioned. "It may be some time before your strengths emerge."

"I want a sword," Tamaes said immediately.

His mentor's eyebrows lifted. "Did the encampment's weapons master already pinpoint your aptitude?"

The boy shuffled his heavy boots. "No, but *you* have a sword."

"As did my mentor." Resting his hand atop auburn hair, Taweel gently urged, "Patience. I wish to see for myself how you fare with ax, bow, spear, and sling. But if a sword is to be your ally, you will receive it from my hands in this place."

138
ADAPTATION

For Tamaes's first flight in his new armor, Taweel was prepared to take it slow. "Can you manage?"

"Fear not!" His apprentice flung himself off the rim, quickly gaining air.

To Taweel's surprise, the boy used the weight of his boots to sling through a twisting flip. "Clearly, my concerns were unfounded."

Omri chittered indulgently.

Taweel swept upward and soared into the lead, modeling the correct wing position to take them higher. Tamaes followed without a wobble, zinging along in the carefree manner of Messengers.

"Watch for more young malakim," Taweel murmured to Omri. "They have been a good influence."

Training was essential, so the return journey became a practical lesson in evasive maneuvers. In other words, a game of chase. Taweel rushed his apprentice, who squeaked like a yahavim before tucking his wings and dropping out of reach.

'He loves you.'

Purple wings shivered, and Taweel's pursuit pattern faltered. "I know it."

'And are known.'

And there it was. Taweel could devote himself to another young life, but not at a distance, unseen and unrequited. Tamaes sought his gaze, heard his voice … and loved him back. God had given Taweel a child who could never be taken away.

140
THRICE BLESSED

Taweel had dawdled so Tamaes could gain confidence. But in the process, the pierced warrior found his own. By the time they strode into the encampment, he was ready. And Tamaes was more than ready.

"Adin!"

Dropping his spear, Adin abandoned his sparring partner and crashed into Tamaes, half-throttling his twin in an affectionate headlock. "You left!"

"I was Sent." Pulling loose, Tamaes straightened. "But I came back."

Adin exclaimed, "You have *armor*!"

"Yes."

"And *boots*!"

Tamaes shyly boasted, "My mentor took me to meet the Forgers."

At this, Adin's attention swung, and happiness suffused his face. "You got *Taweel*!"

141
MOST WELCOME

Adin charged Taweel, who huffed in amusement at the boy's enthusiastic greeting. Ruffling up sleek hair, he said, "Yes, I am gotten. Though usually apprentices are said to belong to their mentors."

"Belonging goes both ways," Adin retorted. "That's what Valerian says."

"That saying is older than Time," countered a lean Guardian with a loose braid of straw-colored hair and a pair of practice spears propped against his shoulder.

"Overseer," Taweel greeted. "We interrupted your lesson."

"In a way most welcome." Valerian rested a hand on Tamaes's shoulder and said, "Everything is in readiness. Our tents will be your shelter."

142
Four Cots

"This way! Hurry up!" urged Adin, who hauled on Taweel's arm.

"Lead on."

The boy darted ahead, then stopped before the centermost structure. "This is ours!"

Hadarim were raised in tents, but not because they needed sleep or shelter. Thanks to humanity, Taweel better understood how these retreats gave a mentor and his apprentice time and space to bond.

At Valerian's invitation, Taweel entered. Tamaes slipped inside and stuck by his side as they peered around. "For us?" he asked eagerly.

"*All* of us," Adin confirmed.

Taweel was pleased with the arrangement. The boys and their brotherhood would remain intact.

143
Song of Dedication

Although Tamaes was eager to begin training in earnest, Taweel delayed. In taking the boy ahead to the Forgers, they'd missed one selection day tradition. And to keep it, they needed a Worshiper. More specifically, Taweel wanted Asaph.

They found the blue-haired angel amidst the candle-trees. "So *this* is what God Most High had in store!"

Tamaes stood as tall as possible. "I have much to learn, and Taweel will teach me."

"As it should be." Asaph knelt before Tamaes and gently took his hands. "But something is lacking. Sing with me?"

The boy whispered, "Can I see your wings?"

144
Vows

Tamaes sighed in delight as Asaph unfurled. Feather-like blades of rainbow light swayed upon threads of lightning, like a thousand tongues of fiery glass. The Worshiper shook out his wings in a harmonious cascade, then began a song all angels knew: the zamarim call to worship.

The young Guardian made it a duet.

Taweel soon added his counterpoint, for the song of dedication was a trio. Vows wove with worship. Promises mingled with praise. He voiced pledges of unity and cooperation in their service to God.

When the last note faded, Asaph concluded, "Amen, amen, and again I say amen."

ARE WE THERE YET

All the solemnity of the occasion was lost when Tamaes immediately turned to his mentor to ask, "*Now* can I start training?"

Asaph hid a smile behind his sleeve, and Taweel sighed. "Start?"

Tamaes nodded. "How else will I get my own sword?"

Taweel blandly pointed out, "Your training *began* when you brought me my sword."

The boy hung his head. "Am I too impatient?"

"*Always* tell me what you hope for, but trust me for the timing."

"I want a sword," he whispered.

Asaph laughed, and Taweel's lips quirked. "It is time I introduced myself to the weapons master."

146
ℒAGGING

The more Taweel watched the boys, the more he worried. Especially for Tamaes. Adin excelled at every task, yet his twin toyed with things. Patient. Unhurried. Behind.

"What is he *doing*?" Taweel muttered to the overseer.

Valerian laughed quietly. "He is testing the balance of his spear."

As Tamaes returned to the pile of spares beside the practice field and chose another, Taweel shuffled his feet. "The boy lacks focus."

"Yet he notices details the others run past." Valerian clapped his shoulder. "Do not complain about traits you yourself emulate, guardian of Weavers, friend of Messengers, and captain of yahavim."

CONSIDERATION

When a new song signaled the next watch, Tamaes started to run after Adin. But all of a sudden, he remembered that he wasn't a newfoundling any longer. He couldn't simply go off and play with Adin. Or go visit Weft. Or challenge the other newfoundlings to a sparring session. An apprentice looked to his mentor first!

Skidding to a stop, Tamaes wheeled so fast, he crashed right into Taweel.

The warrior steadied him. "Did you forget something?"

Tamaes sheepishly admitted, "*You.*"

"We both have new habits to form." Taweel suggested, "Consider me, even as I will consider you."

"Agreed!"

148
REPETITION

"Again."

Tamaes brought the practice sword down against his mentor's blade with less eagerness than his first several whacks. Vibrations rattled up his arms. Was he making *any* progress?

"Again."

He swung and connected with another bone-jarring *clang*. Flexing his fingers, Tamaes adjusted his grip. Then corrected his stance. There was so much to remember.

"Again."

Tamaes knew his arms would ache later on, but his blood sang in his veins. He'd been made for this, and if he endured now, he could offer his strength to God.

Taweel checked, "Do you wish to rest?"

Tamaes shook his head. "Again."

A Friend in Need

Tamaes slipped through Loris's door behind his mentor, then beckoned to Adin. While Taweel and Valerian caught up with the Weaver, the boys cornered their friend.

"Help us?" Tamaes begged.

"Me?" Weft asked, wide-eyed at their hushed urgency. "What's wrong?"

"My arms," Adin groaned. "They hurt."

"And my hands." Tamaes showed blistered palms.

"What can I do?" the Weaver's apprentice asked.

Adin wheedled, "Remember that time when we had our baths here …?"

Weft quickly caught on. "Stone basins *are* heavy."

"Too heavy," grumbled Adin.

Tamaes added, "Please?"

Their friend's eyes shone speculatively. "Do you need help with your hair?"

150
TWISTS AND TURNS

Valerian's story of encampment exploits stuttered to a stop. "Adin?"

Loris murmured, "My, my."

Taweel turned and his eyebrows began a slow ascent. He'd been aware of the scent and splash of water from the inner room. But this?

Tamaes and Adin stood shoulder to shoulder, cheeks pink from fresh washing. Their hair showed a Weaver's workmanship, with braids swirling from nape to crown.

Valerian chose diplomacy. "You boys are wise to consider your options. Many warriors braid or bind their hair."

Weft collapsed into giggles, setting off the other two, and Taweel sighed in relief. They were only playing.

Pushing Boundaries

Now that Taweel was conscious of Tamaes's inquisitive nature, he noticed how often the boy asked him to indulge it. "How did you know there are cherubim encampments?" Taweel asked.

Tamaes blinked. "I did not *know*. I guessed. Was I wrong?"

"No. They also dwell in tents." He nodded toward the territories beyond the districts. "The nearest enclave is that way."

"Can we go?"

Taweel saw no harm in letting Tamaes's curiosity guide their course. "Unfurl your wings. There are no roads into the fringes."

The boy hesitated, "No roads? Do they not like visitors?"

"Let us see for ourselves."

152
ENCLAVE

The enclave's overseer welcomed them and spoke kindly to Tamaes. "We have no newfoundlings in our tents. All our boys are nearing the end of their lessons."

Tamaes spotted several adolescents with long bows. "What happens when there is nothing left to learn?"

Their host leaned down to grip Tamaes's shoulder. "There is *always* something more to learn. And in the fullness of time, you will go to your charge. And we will go with you."

"Cherubim will?"

"You and your mentor will be added to one of our Flights."

"Can I try?"

The cherub winked, straightened, and whistled shrilly.

153

CHERUBIM GAMES

Arrows rained down, but the formation of young cherubim didn't endanger Tamaes. "We are both warriors, but you fight differently."

The overseer explained, "Guardians defend their charges. Protectors engage the enemy."

In this impromptu game, Taweel and five of the enclave's teachers had "captured" Tamaes. Their students formed Flights and rallied to rescue him.

Tamaes understood little of strategy, but when a daring boy dropped from the sky and swathed him in cobalt wings, he knew the game was won.

"Fear not. You are safe," his rescuer said solemnly.

"I will not be afraid." Tamaes shyly added, "Cherubim are *amazing*."

154
In the Armory

Tamaes asked, "What is that?"

"Crossbow." The enclave's weapons master placed it the boy's hands. He cast a sidelong look at Taweel. "Hadarim don't teach archery?"

"We favor close range weapons."

Tamaes struggled to lift the crossbow. "Like this?"

"Almost." Gently correcting the boy's grip, the cherub said, "I do not have a smaller size."

"Oh. Am I too little?"

"Not to learn. Let's take this bow apart and put it back together. Then you'll understand its strengths and limitations." He held Taweel's gaze and added, "When you're older, find me again, and we'll see if your aim is true."

Share and Share Alike

"Where *were* you?"

Tamaes stopped short at Adin's injured tone. "With Taweel. Training."

His friend muttered, "No fair. Taweel is mine, too."

Was he? Things had certainly started out that way, with both boys impressed by the mysterious warrior at Weft's house. But Tamaes was Taweel's apprentice now. His name was under his mentor's hand; Taweel's etched over Tamaes's heart.

Adin said, "Valerian wouldn't let me search, and he had lessons."

"I am here." Tamaes hugged Adin, who had to share his mentor with the whole encampment. "Do you want to spar?"

His twin grinned. "I'll get two spears!"

156
On the Sidelines

Adin was showing an aptitude for the spear. "He is a good match for you," Taweel remarked.

"Hmm," Valerian agreed, his attention fixed on their apprentices. "My mentor was also a spearman."

"And a harpist?"

The lean Guardian tore his eyes from the sparring. "No."

Taweel asked, "How long have you played?"

"A Messenger shoved that harp into my hands shortly after I was pierced. It endured many mournful melodies before I remembered joy." Valerian's gaze flitted to Taweel's shoulder, where Omri gripped his dainty handhold. "Is he your harp?"

Omri patted his cheek, and Taweel grunted. "One of many."

Tamaes wasn't sure how to explain, but he had to try. "May I remain here?"

Taweel looked him up and down. "Did Adin injure you?"

"No. I am well." Tamaes tried again. "But he was sad."

"Adin?"

"Yes. He missed me. And you. Us."

"You *enjoy* our outings."

Tamaes shuffled his feet. "But he was sad."

"Did Adin ask you to stay within the Hedge?"

"Nooo. I am the one asking."

With a soft sigh, Taweel summed it up neatly. "You want to grow up with Adin, not apart from him."

Tamaes flung his arms around Taweel's arm. "May I?"

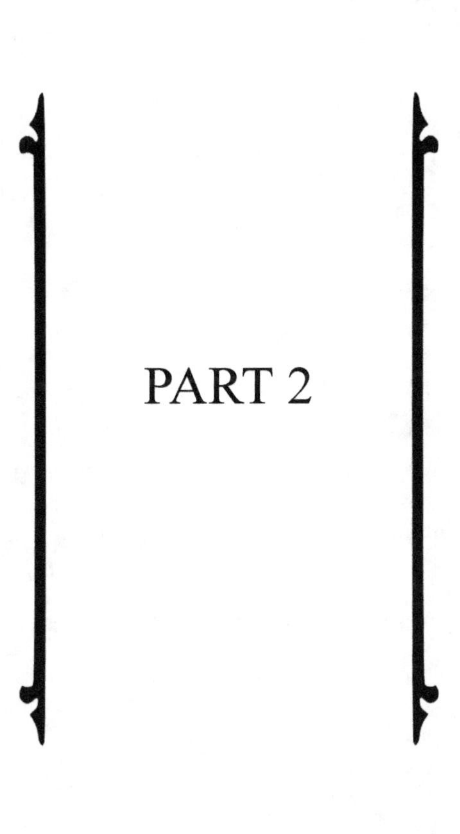

PART 2

Two Guardians paused in the middle of sparring and lowered their weapons. "Would you look at that?"

"Newfoundlings."

"There haven't been any little guys here since we were brought in."

"I know."

The auburn-haired teens leaned against their spears as a line of wide-eyed youngsters trailed by. Adin asked, "Were we ever that puny?"

Tamaes shook his head. "It does not seem possible."

Adin's attention snapped to the Overseer's tent. "Gotta go. Valerian wants me."

Tamaes caught his friend's spear and turned toward the armory, nearly colliding with his own mentor. Taweel gruffly said, "Yes."

"Yes?"

"You were that puny."

159
Consequences

Taweel smiled faintly at the way Tamaes straightened. The top of the boy's head still didn't reach his shoulder. "Are you in a hurry to gain height?"

"Being in between is … difficult."

Bending to catch his apprentice's eye, Taweel asked, "What difficulty have you encountered?"

Tamaes lowered his gaze. "I am unsure."

"And I am your mentor. Can you not confide in me?"

Relief flashed through reddish-brown eyes. Splaying his hand over his breastplate, Tamaes admitted, "Something is stirring. And my wings are restless."

With a grunt, Taweel asked, "Are you sad?"

Tamaes's voice cracked. "How did you know?"

"Come with me."

Tamaes jogged after Taweel, who strode over to Valerian. Newfoundlings surrounded Adin, who cheerfully announced, "And here's Taweel. He teaches sword."

The youngsters stared up at the grim-faced warrior.

Tamaes quickly added, "My mentor is kind. See? Even yahavim love him."

One boy bashfully asked, "Is he hungry?"

"Are you?" Tamaes knelt with Adin and signaled to the little angel. "This is Omri."

Manna and antics distracted all of them, so Tamaes missed what Taweel said to Valerian. He was completely surprised when his mentor hauled him up, tossed him over one shoulder, and carried him away.

161
Provisions for the Journey

"Fear not!" Tamaes waved to the youngsters from over Taweel's broad shoulder, hoping to reassure them. In lower tones, he said, "You have startled them."

"Valerian can explain."

Tamaes tried to wriggle free, but Taweel's grip didn't loosen. "Will *you* explain?"

Taweel only grunted.

He tried again. "Where are we going?"

"Wherever we end up."

Although it wasn't much of an answer, Tamaes was intrigued. This almost sounded like the outings they took when he was newly apprenticed. "How long will we be gone?"

Taweel answered an entirely different question. "God has provided eight newfoundlings. Adin will not be lonely."

PINCH

Taweel was prepared to march his apprentice straight off heaven's threshold, but Tamaes didn't resist.

Instead, the young angel tugged lightly at the chain on Taweel's earring. "You are confused, my mentor. This is Omri's place."

"So it is."

Tamaes smiled. "Am I not your apprentice? I will follow you."

With a soft grunt, Taweel dropped to one knee, letting him down. Taking advantage of the position, the burly angel prodded at the toes of Tamaes's boots. "Your feet have grown. These will pinch soon. We should visit the Forgers."

Restless wings unfurled in a blaze of orange. "Lead on!"

163
SHOOTING STARS

Tamaes didn't like darkness, but he no longer feared its depths. Not when he, Taweel, and Omri carried heaven's brilliance with them. Wings like flames arrowed across the celestial expanse, chasing a purple blur. "Is this the way?" he called.

Taweel wheeled back to circle his apprentice. "That depends on our destination."

Pointing confidently to a cluster of stars, Tamaes said, "We will find a Forge there."

"Are your wings already weary?"

"Not at all."

"That is our destination." His mentor drew his blade and beckoned for Tamaes to ready his spear. "But we will take the long way around."

Twirl.

Sweep.

Thrust.

Even though Tamaes fought confidently with his spear, Taweel kept him on the defensive. Over and over, the younger Guardian was forced to bring up his wings to deflect a ringing blow.

Spin.

Duck.

Slash.

Aerial tactics were Tamaes's favorite. He borrowed from the cherubim's stratagem and the malakim's acrobatics. By adding what he'd learned in the hadarim encampment, he made the battle his own. Unique. Versatile. But frustratingly limited against Taweel's sword.

"This would go better if you also held a spear," he complained.

Taweel smirked. "You would *be* better if you also held a sword."

165

ʟapis ɪnnis Merriel ɴock

The Fourfold were strange, with their feathered wings and hoofed feet. But Tamaes had outgrown his boots several times, and with each return trip to the wheels within wheels, he'd grown closer to the heavenly guard named Lapis Innis Merriel Nock.

"Why do you cling to your spear?" asked the angel with a lion's face.

Tamaes gripped his weapon's smooth haft. "I am Adin's sparring partner."

"Your brother treasures your companionship, but you are not the same."

"Not like you and your brothers."

"We are four and one," Nock agreed. "But you are two, and your paths must be two."

Sentient rings changed their tune, and the Fourfold smiled. Nock spoke first, and as usual, his brothers chimed in. "Tamaes, the opanim have given thought …"

" … to a gift for you."

"Did you forget your …"

" … first love in order to …"

" … please your first friend?" Nock finished.

The angels took his hands and drew him closer to the opanim, whose gyrations slowed enough to reveal a weapon suspended within. Jeweled eyes winked and sparkled as Nock lifted out a sword and presented it to Tamaes.

His gasp became a grunt. "It is *heavy*!"

167

ℓike a Flockmate

Taweel doubted any would fault him. Still, he preferred that God alone bear witness when he fussed like a flockmate. "Is it bright enough?"

Omri hummed contentedly, running tiny hands along the edges of a transparent wing. Starlight brought out hints of colors, as if through delicate prisms.

"Let me see your hair."

The little angel turned his back and chirruped.

Taweel snorted. "You have tangles."

With a grumble-squeak, Omri searched for the offending snarl. His ponytail slipped sideways and came undone.

"Worse and worse."

Omri muttered.

Taweel smiled. "Sorry, friend. My fingers are too big. Shall we find Tamaes?"

168

AND IT WAS GOOD

Omri tilted an elfin ear and peeped.

Taweel heard it, too, and grunted. "He has found us. But what *is* that?"

A faint scrape of metal upon stone brought back memories. He touched the hilt of the sword Tamaes had brought to him so long ago. Cradling Omri to his chest, Taweel started walking. "Tamaes?"

"Here I am!"

His apprentice trundled awkwardly into view, his spear hooked under his arm, its tip dragging along the ground. Taweel should have scolded Tamaes for mistreating a weapon, but the spear's importance swiftly dimmed. "A sword?"

Tamaes nodded.

"Good." Taweel smiled. "*Very* good."

169
GROOMING

"**W**eft has a lighter touch," whispered Tamaes.

Omri blinked up at him, all trust as he helped confine his hair.

Tamaes stole a peek at his mentor. "He seems pleased."

The little angel brightened.

Taweel inspected the newly-forged weapon, testing its heft and edge. Finally, he said, "You used to want a sword. In the beginning."

"Yes." Tamaes ducked his head. "The opanim remembered."

"Will you learn from me?"

"In all things, but especially in this." Tamaes accepted his sword, bracing the heavy blade with both hands. "Only … is it too big?"

Taweel grunted. "You will grow into it."

Tamaes propped his new sword against his shoulder and watched Nock's brothers team up against Taweel. The Fourfold made terrifying sparring partners. Fire-bronzed feathers beat the air. Hooves clattered against stone. They thought as one, moved as one.

Tamaes said, "If we joined Taweel, the sides would be even."

"Impossible," replied Nock. "I cannot fight myself."

"But he cannot win."

"Victory is not his goal."

Which made sense. These weren't enemies. The mock battle flowed like a dance, but Tamaes could tell his mentor fought seriously. "He holds nothing back."

Nock's leonine smile revealed sharp teeth. "Struggle bears good fruit."

171
Now You

Eagle, man, and ox—Nock's brothers opened their circle. "Now you."

Tamaes drew his sword and put his back to Taweel's. Keeping up was a struggle, but working in tandem felt right. "Is this what it will be like?"

Taweel snorted. "The enemy is rarely this polite."

"I meant *this*," Tamaes corrected. "You protecting me. My protecting you."

"Yes." The big warrior spared him a glance. "And together, we will protect the one whose name God places under your hand."

"Soon?"

"Who can say?" Taweel fended off another blow before adding, "It *could* be soon, and I want you ready."

"**R**eady?" asked Taweel.

"Yes." Tamaes closed his eyes and joined the dream. The sound of a harp drew them in, and Valerian came into focus.

He left off strumming. "I was beginning to think you lost your way."

"Not at a–"

Tamaes didn't get to finish, for Adin tackled him. "I thought you were coming home!"

Grinning over the way his best friend's voice cracked, Tamaes said, "We *are*. But Taweel is taking the long way."

"So where are you?"

"Somewhere in the fringes," said Taweel.

"Training?"

"Not exactly." Tamaes traded smiles with his mentor. "Our hosts are Observers."

173
At the Archive

din frowned. "Why Observers?"

"They wished to hear our stories," Tamaes said.

His friend laughed. "*Taweel* tells stories?"

"Short ones." Tamaes peeked at his stoic mentor, who took a seat beside Valerian. "This place is beautiful. The Observers' tower is surrounded by golden flowers."

"Flowers?" Adin rounded on Taweel. "*This* is how you train my brother? By throwing flower petals at him?"

"No. Tamaes is resting."

"An injury?" Concern flitted across Adin's face. "Were you winged or wounded?"

"Nothing like that." Tamaes lifted his hands. "I am quite well."

"Then wh– ?"

Valerian interrupted. "Already?"

Taweel nodded. "He is ready."

Ready or Not

A din demanded, "*What* are you ready for?"

"A test." Tamaes couldn't dredge up a smile. "I must face our enemy."

"A Fallen?" Adin's voice skipped an octave.

Valerian reacted more calmly. "This is the natural progression of training."

"But …!"

"He *is* ready," Taweel repeated, gripping Adin's shoulder. "And I will be with him."

Adin squirmed under the warrior's hand. "If you say Tamaes is ready, then he *is*, but …!"

The mentors exchanged a long look before Valerian asked, "Did you have something to say, apprentice?"

Linking arms with Tamaes, Adin exclaimed, "Shouldn't twins face their first demon together?"

175
TESTING

When the dream ended, Tamaes stayed where he was. Tucking his hands behind his head he gazed quietly toward the white tower rising above the golden flowers that grew up all around them.

Taweel sat up, glancing around until he spotted Omri. The little angel was flying circles around a honeybee.

"Adin was …."

Purple eyes slanted his way. Taweel asked, "Sad?"

Tamaes hummed.

"Facing a Fallen will test your skills, not the bond you share with Adin."

"Yes, I understand. And I am prepared."

Taweel sighed. "But?"

With an apologetic glance, Tamaes said, "I do not think Adin agrees."

176

FACING THE FALLEN

Tamaes followed his mentor through a narrow crevice into a rocky pit. Its sheer sides were like black mirrors, scarred by deep slashes. Light pooled in the center of this prison, but shadows wreathed the perimeter. And from their depths came grinding noises, strange mutters, and the reek of death.

"Wings up," reminded Taweel.

Tightening both hands on his sword hilt, Tamaes arched his wings defensively. They trembled along with his heart. What would the Fallen be like?

He glanced at Taweel, who calmly said, "When you are ready."

But Tamaes never made it to *ready*. The demon attacked first.

177
VERBAL ASSAULT

Taweel longed to draw his sword, but he held back. This was Tamaes's fight.

The Fallen sized up his cornered opponent and sneered. "Do the stars still excrete innocents for us to mangle?"

To Taweel's relief, Tamaes didn't answer. Nothing good ever came of reasoning with demons.

"Foolish pup." Hate echoed against the pit's bleak walls. "Your mentor cast you at my feet. I can help you Fall further."

Taweel's jaw tightened, but with every oozing suggestion, he could see Tamaes's resolve strengthen. Then the boy gave the only correct answer to the bilge of lies. He swung his sword.

UNYIELDING

Tamaes managed to drive his opponent into a corner, but Valerian had lectured them over and over. The Fallen had nothing left to lose. In their desperation, they became doubly dangerous.

"Yield!" Tamaes snapped, leveling his sword at the demon's throat.

With a scratchy laugh, he countered, "Why? To impress your mentor?"

"To … to end the test."

"Did no one tell you?" jeered the demon. "*Nothing* ends here." And he sprang.

Tamaes's blade sliced the Fallen's shoulder, but his enemy pushed forward, heedless of his wound. He didn't stop until his teeth were buried in the young Guardian's arm.

179
ONCE BITTEN

A sharp blow from Taweel's sword hilt robbed the demon of consciousness.

Into the sudden stillness, Tamaes groaned, "He *bit* me."

Taweel knelt to pry the slumped demon's jaws from his apprentice's arm. He dragged the limp figure to the pit's other side, then returned to Tamaes. "Can you stand?"

"I failed." Luminous droplets welled up between the youth's fingers as he clutched at torn flesh. He whispered, "I am sorry."

"Do not apologize." Taweel hauled Tamaes up, then collected his sword. "The test fulfilled its purpose."

"*What* purpose?" In bitter tones, he asked, "Pain?"

"No," Taweel gently corrected. "Wisdom."

Ready for More

Tamaes threw an arm over his eyes while Taweel wrapped his wound, but Omri pushed and pried. With a sigh, Tamaes came out of hiding. The little angel peeped and petted the crease between his eyebrows.

"You are too quiet. He is worried," said Taweel.

"I would rather hear *your* thoughts."

His mentor grunted. "You expected too much from your enemy. A friend might yield in a fair fight, but an enemy will drag you down with him."

"Truly."

Taweel took his hand. "Your training changes shape from here. I need two things from you."

"What?"

"Your trust. And courage."

181
SCARS

"Without a Caretaker's intervention, this will scar."

"I do not mind," said Tamaes. "*You* have scars."

"Many."

"Do you remember how you received each one?"

Taweel brought up his wings, tucking them around his apprentice. "Vividly."

Safely swathed in their shelter, Tamaes asked, "Were they mistakes?"

"Mostly."

Touching a patch of puckered skin on his mentor's forearm, he murmured, "Valerian calls scars lessons."

"If so, they are learned too late."

Tamaes tilted his head back and searched Taweel's face. "Maybe the lessons are for *me*."

Taweel grunted. "Choose one, and we will see if you can learn from my mistake."

PLANNING AHEAD

Amidst anecdotes of rough patches in Taweel's training, his wings did their good work, hastening the healing of his apprentice's injury.

"I see my mistake." Tamaes scratched under the edge of his bandage. "Too much cherubim. Not enough hadarim."

"We *are* defenders."

"Next time, I will defend you. Or Omri."

"Good plan." Taweel was even more certain Tamaes was ready. "We should take a trip into humankind's realm."

"Why?"

"Tracking, mostly. Although someone we know has been Sent into Time. He would welcome a visit."

Tamaes must have guessed their destination, for his eyes took on a shine. "Good plan!"

183
TRACKING

Tamaes throttled his sword hilt as he scanned the barren landscape. "We are exposed. If any Fallen are near, they must see us."

"And we will see them," Taweel said. "With no danger of ambush, you can focus."

His grip eased. Trekking up a rocky slope, he found nothing but spiky weeds and fitful winds. "Demons do not leave tracks," Tamaes murmured, half to himself. "What am I looking for?"

"Destruction. Confusion. An unholy stench. An off-key clam–"

Bent figures appeared on the neighboring rise and flung garbled accusations that set Tamaes's teeth on edge.

Taweel sighed. "And lies."

Time passed with startling speed upon the earth. While the sun swung low in a vivid blaze of colors, Tamaes stood in awe.

The sky slowly filled with stars before Taweel broke the silence. "Night makes the Fallen bold."

So far, the only enemies they'd glimpsed were skulkers and sneaks with no interest in a confrontation. Tamaes was more interested in the changing sky. Pointing to a twinkling cluster near the horizon, he said, "Nock is there."

Taweel tapped his shoulder and gestured to the faint glimmer of torches along the walls of a large human city. "Asaph is there."

185
JOIN THE THRONG

Tamaes loitered on a promontory to watch the morning sky fill with blush and blue, and Taweel let him. Hadn't he done the same when he was new to such things? The sky was thick with angels on more urgent business then theirs. So when his apprentice jumped down to rejoin him, Taweel said, "We will walk."

"So many people." Tamaes sidestepped donkey dung and peeked inside a creaking cart.

"They are here for the festival," Taweel said flatly.

Mahogany eyes swiveled to the limestone walls of their destination. "The holy mountain."

"The footstool of heaven. The royal city. Jerusalem."

186
To Walk Unseen

Taweel set aside his inner turmoil in order to guide his apprentice in the correct direction. Their path was as sure as Sending, but Tamaes dawdled.

"They are building a temple?"

"For many years," Taweel replied. "The task was given to Israel's king by his father."

Tamaes paused on a staircase. "They cannot see us."

"No."

"Humans are smaller than I expected."

Taweel huffed. "They are weak, so we are strong."

They reached a wide courtyard before Tamaes finally asked, "Why is Asaph *here*?"

"He was Sent to live as a man among men. Our friend has become a Graft."

187
Disguised

Tamaes didn't realize that he was looking at Asaph until Taweel made a soft noise of surprise.

Omri shed light on the situation by buzzing over to a man bent over a scroll. His hair was black, and his eyes were brown, but there was no mistaking his sleepy smile.

Asaph embraced Tamaes, then placed his hand over Taweel's heart. "I'm surprised you didn't wait until after the festival. How are you faring, friend?"

Taweel sighed.

"What do you mean?" asked Tamaes.

"This is Passover," Asaph explained. "The celebration of Israel's deliverance falls upon the day your mentor was pierced."

188
In Remembrance

For a long time, Tamaes had thought of the heavy silver ring piercing Taweel's ear as Omri's handhold. But that *wasn't* why it hung there. The true reason still flitted through his mentor's eyes, the shadow of a memory. A lost love.

Tamaes whispered, "Does it still hurt?"

"Only when I remember."

Asaph smiled bemusedly. "That often?"

Taweel's low voice held deep conviction. "I will never forget."

"Tonight will be for remembering," promised Asaph. "Join us for evensong."

"Us?"

Pushing aside once-blue hair, the disguised Worshiper revealed an ear cuff. "My new apprentice and I will lead you into worship."

Tamaes blurted, "Can I meet him?"

"If we can *find* him." Asaph explained, "He chases down melodies for me, and with the city filling up for Passover, songs are everywhere."

As they strolled through a columned hallway, Tamaes hummed along with a group of singers somewhere beyond the palace walls.

"Catchy, isn't it? King David's psalms are truly inspired."

Taweel's fingers tapped his thigh, and he hummed a harmony line.

When a new sound reached them, Asaph's pace quickened. "There! He's in the throne room again. That boy's become very attached."

"To the king?" Taweel asked.

"To the king's *harp*."

King Solomon

They slipped into a room filled with natural beauty and grand extravagances. Potted palms. Caged birds. Ripe fruit. Hammered gold. Busy men. Lovely women. And in their midst reclined Israel's king.

Tamaes quietly asked, "Is that David?"

"No, Solomon is David's son." Asaph smiled indulgently. "He calls my apprentice 'little David'."

Despite the buzz of conversation, the king's attention was clearly fixed upon the sweet notes coming in an endless cascade from the boy who cradled a lap harp with the distinctive carving of a lion's head upon its frame.

Asaph added, "Solomon trusts his father's instrument to no other."

191
KEEPER OF SONGS

When evening brought an end to Asaph's duties, he slipped out of Time and guise. Tamaes felt more at ease with Worshiper now that his hair was blue again.

Asaph explained, "I was chosen by King Solomon to compile a treasury of psalms. David's words shall not pass from memory."

Tamaes tweaked the sleeve of Asaph's apprentice, who seemed to be more or less his own age. "Could you teach me one?"

The young Worshiper, whose dark eyes and black ringlets remained even *without* his disguise, scooted closer and offered a single nod. "Most assuredly. As many as you like."

Tamaes found humanity fascinating. From Jerusalem's walls, he watched their lives unfold. Families and faith. Priests and prayers. Songs and sacrifices. Laughter and lessons. Taweel attempted to turn their loitering into practical training on the formation and flexibility of Hedges, but Tamaes interrupted.

"Are you sad?"

"In part," Taweel replied. "Is that what has distracted you?"

"I want to understand."

"You *will* … when your own Sending comes."

Tamaes dared to ask, "Can you show me where she lived?"

His mentor looked away. "Centuries have passed. Much will have changed."

"Please?"

With a sigh, Taweel unfurled his wings. "Follow me."

193
FOLLOW ME

Memories weighed heavily on Taweel as he struck out across the sea. Measured wingbeats barely kept him aloft. Ponderous. Pondering. What was the use in showing Tamaes where he'd served? Nothing remained. And yet Taweel was as sure of his course as a migrating bird.

A piece of his heart must have remained in Egypt.

"Too slow!"

Taweel was yanked from his ruminations by Tamaes, who zipped beneath him with an aerobatic twist and a small wave.

"Faster!" the boy urged. "Higher!"

Meeting his apprentice's challenge with a powerful surge, Taweel chased another piece of his heart into the sky.

One Thing Remains

"The terrain changes the threat," Taweel explained. "When I was here, the Fallen used to ooze up out of the river, whispering nightmares and stealing hope. Much different than those valleys, where every crevice and gulley is enough t– "

Tamaes halted the lecture by driving both fists into his mentor's breastplate. "*Stop!*"

Taweel grunted in surprise.

"You are rambling." The boy's eyes flashed. "You do *not* ramble."

Silence echoed in the silted plain abandoned by everything—even the river.

Finally, Taweel said, "There is nothing left."

"Teach me *this*," Tamaes demanded. "Teach me how to love my charge forever."

195
HARD TO IMAGINE

"I want to train," Tamaes said.

"I cannot teach you to love … any more than I can teach myself to *un*love." Taweel flicked his apprentice's breastplate, right over his heart. "We were made for this, Tamaes."

"What if I fall short?"

Taweel shook his head. "You cannot."

Tamaes's boots scuffed the earth. "But I cannot imagine it. I do not understand!"

"Which part."

"This girl. You love her."

"I do."

"Even though she is gone?"

"Even so."

"And you will never forget."

"So it seems."

Tamaes frowned. "Even though it makes you sad."

"Your turn will come," promised Taweel.

196
HOMESICK

A new restlessness stirred in Tamaes's wings. Omri noticed first. The little angel flitted to his shoulder and crawled under draping layers of fiery light, pushing and peeping as if in answer to the subtle shift.

Tamaes drew up his wing, creating a pocket for his friend. "Is this a new game?"

But he couldn't camouflage the truth from Taweel. Once his mentor's attention fixed on something, it was a force worth reckoning.

Taweel asked, "Why does wistfulness whisper through your wings?"

Tamaes summed up his longing as best he could. "I think … I am ready to go home."

197
Mutual

Heaven's light washed over Taweel and Tamaes, lending strength to weary wings. They climbed to dazzling heights, a shout on their lips, a song in their hearts. And God welcomed them by name.

Tamaes asked, "Can we hurry?"

"Do you know the way?" Taweel checked, for they were still some distance from their own district.

With a short laugh, his apprentice arrowed away, making for a distant spark of color.

Catching up to his apprentice, Taweel squinted at the oncoming blaze. A swift, solitary angel. "No one flies this high except Messengers and …."

" … and those who rejoice!"

WITHOUT RESERVATION

Tamaes and Adin collided with a *crack* of breastplates and boisterous greetings. Tangled wings sent them tumbling, and Taweel lunged when it became apparent that neither boy intended to let go. Dropping beneath the twins, Taweel hauled them into his arms … and grunted. These two were pushing his limits.

The big warrior barely prevented them from careening into an unfamiliar district. Instead, the three of them ended as a heap in some meadow.

Then Adin's arms were around Taweel's neck, a kiss found his cheek, and teary laughter was in his ear. "I missed you so much! Welcome home!"

199
Catching Up

They walked the rest of the way home. But not directly.

Every open meadow and empty garden offered an excuse to linger.

Adin teased Omri and tickled the little angel's toes.

Taweel let Adin borrow his sword so he could spar with his twin.

Tamaes learned the names of all the newfoundlings in Valerian's encampment.

As their stories grew longer, the distance between them dwindled away.

Shared beginnings.

Overlapping ideas.

Frequent laughter.

And songs.

Together, Tamaes and Adin conquered any awkwardness that came with new beginnings. By the time Taweel led them to Loris's door, they were back in unison.

While Tamaes and Adin regaled Weft, Loris led Taweel to a quieter corner. For many moments, the only sound was the slip of bronze thread through soft raiment. "So Tamaes asked to come home?"

Taweel grunted.

"And you came here."

Thick brows drew together.

Loris helpfully added, "Instead of the encampment."

"Do you mind?"

The Weaver laughed. "I am delighted beyond words, but … there is *this* to consider."

He lifted the tunic, and Taweel recognized his own past, his present, and a future he hadn't expected.

Confirmation came from God Himself. *'Child of Light, I have need of you.'*

201
THUNDERSTRUCK

Tamaes sat quietly, enjoying Adin's bold way of speaking and Weft's giggles. But a noise snatched his attention, and he shot to his feet. The sound had been smaller than one of Omri's squeaks, but Tamaes was certain it had come from his mentor. Not a grunt. Not a groan. It had been more like a whine or a whimper.

Taweel sat in the corner, a crumpled tunic in his big hands, a stunned expression on his face. He lifted his eyes and struggled to find words.

Tamaes hurried to Taweel's side and knelt. "What has happened?"

"I am Sent."

202
TAWEEL'S SENDING

"Sent?" Tamaes glanced from face to face, searching for some hint to his mentor's dismay. Surely God would not Send Taweel away from him. "If you are Sent, we will go."

Adin said, "*We* are the ones waiting for our Sending. Apprentices go, not mentors!"

Which was entirely true. Tamaes's confusion deepened, and he quietly demanded. "Why are you sad?"

Taweel winced and looked to Loris.

The Weaver gently extracted the tunic from Taweel's hands and displayed it to the three boys. "This is cause for rejoicing."

Weft interpreted the new row of stitching first and gasped. "It says *Overseer*."

A voice carried from the front of the Weaver's house. "Loris, Weft, is Adin here?"

Loris hurried out and returned with Valerian, who stopped short. The tension drained from his posture, and he relaxed into a faint smile. "So this is why you left."

"I was Sent," Adin said.

"This time." Valerian turned his attention to Tamaes. "Welcome home, young explorer."

Taweel stood awkwardly by, wondering if it was his place to speak, but when he clasped Valerian's hand, the current overseer registered surprise. Taweel murmured, "I am Sent."

Valerian's grip tightened. "As am I. May I see your blade?"

ETCHINGS

Taweel slowly unsheathed his sword. Even though he knew what he would find, his eyes widened at the change God had wrought. The bared blade was covered with loops and scrolls, an intricate tracery that spelled out his expanded responsibility.

Tamaes leaned closer, touching the pretty whorls. He murmured, "Adin just taught me these names."

Valerian loosed his spear and ran a hand down its haft. Intricate carvings had vanished, leaving smooth wood. "They are no longer under my hand."

Adin lit up. "Do you realize what this *means*?"

Taweel grunted, but Valerian said it plainly. "We are trading places."

205
What it Means

"Bring the young ones here," Loris suggested.

"I'll go!" Adin hooked Tamaes's arm. "*We'll* go!"

Tamaes went along with it, as he usually did when it came to Adin's ideas.

Halfway to the encampment, his twin blurted, "I'm sorry."

"Why?"

His twin searched his face. "You haven't realized what this means?"

Tamaes *did*. "God has added to Taweel's responsibilities."

"What it means *for you*." Adin's voice softened. "We'll be trading places."

"Taweel is my mentor; Valerian is yours. That will not change."

"I can finally go, and you're stuck." Adin explained, "Plus, if Taweel is Overseer, you *can't* be Sent."

   Tried and True

BIG BROTHER

"A din! Adin!" Eight boys abandoned their practice weapons to crowd around the teen.

Tamaes hung back, but Adin dragged him forward. "Look what I brought!"

Gasps and shy glances were followed by a swift migration as newfoundlings hemmed in Tamaes. Questions came thick and fast.

"Is he Tamaes?"

"Are you our big brother's twin?"

"Did you bring Omri?"

A small boy with lavender curls fit his hand into Tamaes's and asked, "Can you stay?"

"Yes, he'll stay!" Adin's voice rang with authority. "Valerian sent me to fetch you! We're going to welcome Taweel and Tamaes with songs, so line up!"

207
Inner Dialogue

Adin collected his mentor's harp, then led the march out of the encampment. The newfoundlings queued up two by two, with Tamaes as rear guard. He was surprised to learn that this was their first trip into the Weavers' district. *You did not introduce them to Weft?*

His twin glanced over his shoulder. *Why would I do that?*

Tamaes blinked.

Adin rolled his eyes. *I share everything I have with everyone that enters the encampment, including my mentor. Loris's place was my secret.* Facing forward again, he squared his shoulders. *At least when you have a secret, you have something.*

SHARE EVERYTHING

Taweel wanted to cherish this responsibility as a gift from God, but there were consequences. Hadn't Tamaes recently expressed his longing to be Sent?

"They're back!" Weft called.

While Valerian introduced the newfoundlings to the Weavers, Taweel drew Tamaes aside. In the alcove where they'd first met, he lamely announced, "I am Sent."

Tamaes nodded pensively.

Emotion hoarsened Taweel's voice. "I cannot often leave. Neither will you, bec–"

"Because we are their home." Tamaes placed his hand over Taweel's heart and cracked a smile. "When I am Sent, you will be my support. Until then, I will be yours."

209
Trusting and Sending

"May it be so." Taweel sat heavily on the cot. "I am grateful for your trust."

Tamaes dropped to a seat beside him. Leaning back on his arms, he stared up through the tumble of vines that dappled the alcove with shadows. "This is better."

"Than what?"

With a faraway look in his eyes, the teen said, "I stayed because Adin was sad. I left because I was sad. But those things changed. I do not think this will."

"This is a Sending."

"And you are *glad*." A slow smile warmed Tamaes's whole expression, and he repeated, "This is better."

Bringing Back Memories

The curtain swayed, and three little boys peered through the gap they'd made—one with short lavender curls, one with a puff of silvery down, and one with two molasses brown knobs. Omri dove at them, flying in excited circles and trilling.

Tamaes murmured, "He *attacked* us."

Taweel grunted, then called, "Will you accept Omri's invitation, or is your courage lacking?"

A grin. A scuffle. A rush. Tamaes chuckled, but his thoughts dwelt on the sour note that had rung with Adin's words earlier. Jealousy? Resentment? Would they creep in now that these children vied for Taweel's time and attention?

211
In Common

"**I** am Bern," said the boy whose knobs of hair made him look like a cub. He pulled his silver-haired friend forward. "And this is Taji."

"I can unfurl now," Taji shyly shared. "I was last."

"And well worth the wait!" exclaimed Adin, who leaned into the alcove. "He is sunlight through ice, a yellow diamond set in silver."

Tamaes blinked at the analogies. Had Valerian taken Adin into creation after all?

The boy with lavender curls said, "I'm Jacinto. Can you be our brother, too?"

Adin beamed. "He *has* to be! Because *I'm* the one who named you all."

In Loris's garden, Valerian called over the newfoundlings one by one. Quiet words. Calm answers. Warm smiles. He explained everything with such poise. "Bern, this is Taweel, the encampment's new overseer." Valerian guided the young Guardian's hands into Taweel's and added, "We are in his care."

This boy's grip was strong, his gaze trusting. But like the others, his eyes soon strayed to Taweel's shoulder.

Omri chirruped, as if offering his opinion on the proceedings.

"Bern." Taweel called back the boy's attention and made the expected response—short, gruff, yet earnest in every regard. "My tents will be your shelter."

213
WOBBLE

Back in the encampment, Tamaes ducked into their tent and felt welcome. "It is the same."

Adin shook his head in amazement. "Of *course* it's the same. Nothing changes here."

"We do," Tamaes countered. "You have."

"I've *improved*! Isn't that the point?" Adin flopped onto his cot. "But why are you carrying a sword? You were finally getting good with a spear!"

"This weapon suits me better."

"Show me."

Tamaes unsheathed his new blade. Struggling with its heft, he quickly adopted a two-handed grip.

Adin laughed and bounded up. "Come on. I know a good exercise for building arm strength."

TRIED AND TRUE

A GOOD PLACE

 Brotherhood with Adin had shaped Tamaes's whole life. He'd always had someone to chase after, to learn from, to love. Following Adin's lead came naturally … until the moment his twin entered the stone pavilion beyond the encampment.

"What are you *doing*?" Tamaes whispered.

"I know a good place to train," Adin said.

Tamaes shifted uneasily. "I cannot go into Time without Taweel."

"Wrong." Adin gestured to the ring set into the floor. "Heaven is no prison. The way is open."

"Y-you do this often?"

"It's like Taweel always said. Are we not Guardians?" Adin laughed. "Where is your courage?"

215
FLYING SOLO

Tamaes wasn't sure how Adin could have so wildly misinterpreted his meaning. Picking his way back through their exchange, he acknowledged, "Heaven is no prison."

"Then let's go!"

Holding his ground, Tamaes asked, "Does Valerian know?"

"If he has an opinion about my private training, he's kept it to himself."

When had Adin become so skilled at evasion? Tamaes's frown deepened. "He does not know."

Adin sighed gustily. "He *suspects*. But I'm careful!"

To Tamaes's increasing dismay, he couldn't tell if Adin meant he was careful while he was alone … or if he was careful not to be caught.

COUNTERBALANCE

"This isn't like you!"

Tamaes kept his eyes forward, his feet moving. "In what way?"

Adin talked faster. "You trust me. We're friends!"

"We *are* friends. But I cannot leave."

"But I just proved you *could*!" argued Adin.

"And I just pledged Taweel my support. Would you make my promise a lie?"

Adin jumped in front of Tamaes. "Then promise *me* something."

"If I can."

"I saved up this secret to share with you. Keep it for me?"

Tamaes slowly countered, "Stay with me. From now on."

Adin pulled his twin into a fierce embrace. "Of course," he promised. "Always."

Valerian introduced Taweel to the prospective mentors who'd begun arriving. "Our newfoundlings have found their wings. Selection is not far off."

Taweel grunted, but when Dorum stepped forward, he grunted again. "You returned?"

"I am *still* here." Dorum smiled blandly. "Valerian asked me to stay on even though I was not given a new apprentice."

"Naturally." Valerian leaned against his spear. "I needed a swordsmanship teacher."

"I am also a prospective." Dorum touched his armored chest, quietly adding, "If God allows, I feel ready to write another name here."

Mirroring his old mentor's gesture, Taweel said, "May it be so."

218

LITTLE BROTHERS

"What else?" asked Bern, who hung from Tamaes's arm.

Jacinto skipped ahead, then turned. "Where is your favorite place?"

"The forges."

"Because of the stars?" asked Jacinto.

"Because of the swords?" asked Taji.

"Because of my friend. Nock and his three brothers are one of the Fourfold."

"Can we?" asked Bern.

"You will see for yourself when you are fitted for boots."

"No!" exclaimed the boy with knobbed hair. "There are four of us!"

"We can be our own Fourfold!" agreed Jacinto.

Tamaes gave in with a smile. Hadn't he played at Flights and Hedges when he was their age?

219
WORTHY

Tamaes barely made it to Taweel's side before evensong began.

"I nearly sent Omri after you."

"I did not stray far."

Taweel lifted a wing, making room for Tamaes. When three newfoundlings crowded close as well, bushy brows lifted.

Tamaes whispered, "We are a Fourfold."

Taweel scooped up Bern and Taji, and Tamaes pulled Jacinto onto his lap. Tucked under purple wings, the trio offered praise that was pure and sweet.

Taweel caught Tamaes's eye over their heads, and with a look, he said much without saying anything. Gratitude. Approval. Trust.

More than ever, Tamaes was glad he hadn't strayed.

220

GUESTS FROM THE FRINGES

Tamaes's attention was caught by a group of cherubim who spiraled to a neat landing in the middle of the encampment's training ground. Recognizing the enclave's weapons master, he hurried to greet the warrior. "But … why are you here?"

"Your overseer invited us." Cherubim scanned the surrounding tents as they unslung assorted weapons.

These visitors looked ready for war. Or a skirmish. Tamaes brightened. "Will you train with us?"

With a nod, the cherub offered a crossbow. "You have grown, Tamaes. Your mentor thinks you are ready to try your hand. Shall we see if your aim is true?"

Taweel scanned collar stitching, quickly tallying eight middlings, four minders. A training Flight.

Omri launched himself at the newcomers. Or possibly Tamaes, who was already in the cherubim's midst. Following the little angel made it easier for Taweel to step past his innate shyness, but he didn't get far.

The yahavim pulled up and zinged sideways, betraying the hiding place of five wide-eyed newfoundlings.

Unfurling, Taweel let his wing brush over the youngsters in playful invitation. Without hesitation, they crowded around his knees, hampering steps that gained new confidence.

Every Guardian was at his best when he became someone's shelter.

LEAD ME NOT

Tamaes felt a tug on his little finger and found Jacinto at his side. The boy asked, "Protectors?"

"Yes." Nodding toward the warriors who were unpacking quivers of arrows, various bows, and targets, he explained, "We older ones will train with them."

"What about me?"

Tamaes ruffled Jacinto's lavender curls. "When you are taller."

Going up on tiptoe, the boy asked, "How *much* taller?"

Adin sauntered past, Taji riding on his shoulders. "Only one way to find out! Let's ask!"

"Follow us!" urged Bern, who loved dares.

As Jacinto chased after them, Tamaes pressed his hand over an uneasy heart.

223
GREAT AND SMALL

Taweel's conference with Dorum and Valerian was interrupted by Adin. "These newfoundlings are eager to learn!"

Bern nodded. "To get stronger."

"Can we?" asked Taji.

Jacinto caught the trailing edge of Taweel's wing. "Am I too little?"

Taweel dropped to one knee. "It was not so long ago that Adin and Tamaes were your size."

Dorum added, "And I remember when Taweel was Adin's size."

The newfoundlings ogled their overseer's impressive physique, and Bern finally asked, "Will I be as big as you?"

"Probably, but there are more important matters than stature."

Dorum nodded. "Be faithful as God is faithful."

A soft sound sent a tremor through Taweel's wings, and he turned to find Tamaes standing slightly apart, speaking softly to Omri. Extricating himself from the others, Taweel hurried over. "Something is amiss."

"I agree."

Taweel's mouth turned down, and his wings came up. "Where?"

Tamaes relaxed into a smile. "I am uninjured."

"You are distressed."

"Not here. Not now." Tamaes glanced in the direction of the weapons master, who was organizing Flights for a skirmish. "Later?"

"Can it keep that long? The cherubim will be with us through several watches."

Tamaes nodded. "I will be waiting."

"As will I."

225
HIERARCHIES

While the newfoundlings collected stray arrows, Taweel showed them how to position their wings to shield their backs. Tamaes's trio stuck closest, which reminded Taweel of something. "Did you give up your game of Fourfold with Tamaes?"

"No," the boys chorused.

Taweel pointed out, "You were with Adin instead."

Jacinto said, "Tamaes is our Fourfold brother."

Taji nodded. "He will return to us."

Something prompted Taweel to ask, "What about Adin?"

Bern patiently explained, "Adin is our leader."

"Is he?" Taweel frowned thoughtfully. "Is he a good leader?"

"He tells us stories."

"He hears our songs."

"He takes us along."

Think the Best

A fresh volley of arrows sent Bern, Taji, and Jacinto scurrying, and Taweel kept half an eye on them. So Adin was their leader? Hardly surprising. Playing at Flights and Hedges was a normal part of a warrior's early years. Taweel was grateful to Adin for taking the newfoundlings under his wing. Was this why he'd been chosen as Valerian's apprentice? To help the overseer nurture young ones?

'No.'

Taweel went still at the solemnity in that one syllable.

God's answer was reinforced by a soft, "No."

He turned to find a Messenger standing by. Some might say *the* Messenger.

227
Private Audience

What was one of heaven's princes doing on an archery range? Feet bare. Wings furled. Vulnerable to stray arrows. Taweel quickly stepped between his unannounced guest and a potential misfire. "You should take more care, Gabriel," he said gruffly. "Our apprentices are inexperienced with the bow."

"Lend me the shelter of your wings, Taweel."

He lifted his wings higher, creating a canopy.

"This would be a good time to *enfold*." Gabriel smiled and stepped closer. "We need to talk."

Without question, Taweel stretched up and out, then twisted his wings together, cocooning the archangel in a swirl of purple light.

Tamaes had done well enough with the crossbow while his boots were on the ground, but handling the weapon midair was challenging. He studied the cherubim closely, imitating their wing positions. Full extension. Rising breezes. Small adjustments.

Adin shouted, "*Now* you're getting it!"

Tamaes's heart soared, and he checked to see if Taweel was watching. But his mentor's wings were wrapped tight as a flower bud. Was one of the newfoundlings injured? Tamaes dropped from the sky. Bright as flames. Swift as light. Sure as Sending. Because Taweel needed him.

Calling out with his thoughts, Tamaes exclaimed, *"I am here!"*

229
Interruption

"*No need to shout.*" The amiable voice in Tamaes's mind held laughter. "*Your mentor is here. As am I.*"

Hands that had been desperately seeking a seam in Taweel's wings stilled. A Messenger? Stepping back, Tamaes murmured, "I apologize for interrupting."

Folds parted, and Omri zipped out to circle Tamaes's head. Taweel's other companion beckoned. "Join us."

Tamaes hadn't seen this particular Messenger in ages, so he was momentarily distracted by the fact that he'd grown taller than the archangel.

Gabriel laughed and took him by the elbow, drawing him in. "Fear not, Tamaes. I'm here to deliver an invitation."

A Taste of Time

"Every so often, heaven opens, and angels fill the skies." In the enclosed space created by Taweel's wings, Gabriel gestured broadly. "For many young angels, it's their first glimpse of Creation."

Taweel grunted. "I have neither seen nor heard of this … *event*."

"Until now, only cherubim and seraphim were Sent."

"But now?" asked Tamaes.

"Hadarim and malakim will join the chorus."

Tamaes glanced uncertainly at his mentor. If *every* Guardian was included, why would Gabriel issue a personal invitation?

"When?" asked Taweel.

"The interval is upon us; prepare your newfoundlings." Gabriel beamed. "They will soon receive their first Sending!"

231
Master's Call

Tamaes clearly remembered his first Sending. Called by a name known only to God. Entrusted with a part in His plans. Allowed to share something precious with his twin.

Under cover of song, Tamaes whispered, "Soon?"

Taweel's gaze slanted his way, and his lips quirked.

The moment came as the last notes of evensong faded. Bern leapt to his feet. Jacinto gasped, and Taji's eyes took on a telltale shine. As all the newfoundlings reacted, their teachers traded knowing looks.

Tamaes nudged his mentor. "My first Sending was to *you*."

Taweel's big hand dropped comfortably onto his head. "I remember."

PREPARE FOR DEPARTURE

Taweel didn't realize he was glowering until a newfoundling's wings curled defensively. "Peace, Jacinto. Did I frighten you?"

"You are fierce."

"My ferocity is for those who might try to harm you."

"I know it." Yet the boy's wings trembled.

Taweel shot a pleading look in Tamaes's direction, but Dorum intercepted it and hurried over. Kneeling before Jacinto, Taweel's former mentor said, "Demons and darkness are not the only things beyond heaven's threshold."

"I know it, but …"

Dorum opened his arms. "We are Sent into the same sky. Stay with me."

Taweel turned to the whole group. "Pair off!"

233
WEIGHT OF RESPONSIBILITY

Tamaes slipped to his mentor's side. "Why has your face turned to stone? Is the danger so great?"

"Who can say?"

Touching Taweel's arm, he said, "Only God. And you recently entertained His Messenger."

"Not here. Not now."

"Later," he agreed, hoping for *soon*.

A purple wing drew around Tamaes's shoulders. "Who will you guide this night?"

"I am with Bern; Adin has Taji."

Taweel said, "I have much to oversee. Keep an eye on Adin for me."

"Valerian will be with us."

"Even so. Stay close to your brother."

Tamaes whispered, "Why?"

Shaking his head, Taweel gruffly answered, "Please."

Thousands upon Thousands

The Guardians of Taweel's encampment flew in such tight formation, the edges of their wings brushed together.

"Is *this* night?" asked Bern.

Tamaes chuckled. "Not in the usual sense. Taweel, can we fly higher?"

"This way." Taweel led them on rising currents through the ranks of cherubim and seraphim, malakim and hadarim who flooded the sky. Their weaving course carried them steadily higher, until they crested the dazzling multitude, giving their newfoundlings their first glimpse of a sky strewn with countless stars.

Bern gasped, and Tamaes whispered, "See the work of His hands. Day *and* night—God called them good."

235
DAYBREAK

The newfoundlings found their confidence and unfurled their wings, and Taweel set a pace they could match. Tamaes swooped and rolled like a Messenger, making Bern laugh.

"Why are the stars fading?" the boy asked.

"We have been flying east. Night will end with morning."

Suddenly, Adin pointed, then dove lower, and Taji chased after him.

"Adin!" shouted Taweel. "Rise! *Now*!"

Black darts sprayed upward, and Taji's wings crumpled. As the boy tumbled, Adin lunged after him, catching his outstretched hand. Tamaes's stomach dropped as Adin hastily wrapped his wings around Taji before they crashed into the dense forest below.

Little Boy Lost

Taweel hit the ground running.

Jeers littered the heavy stillness of the old woods, which reeked of demons. The burly warrior battered his way past a few stragglers, homing in on the clamor of battle. "Adin!"

"Fear not, Taweel! I am here!"

Adin made an arresting sight. Fearless. Flawless. Ferocious. He fought with a smile on his face, as if daring his enemies to approach the crumpled bundle of gold between his feet. Taji.

Valerian dropped through the canopy of trees in a rush of green wings, spear flashing. Adin made room, and they formed their Hedge. Three against twenty.

237
FOCUS

"Enough," growled Taweel.

Valerian brushed aside another volley of darts. "Agreed."

The blunt end of Adin's spear connected with a skull, rendering his attacker senseless. Kicking the demon aside, Adin asked, "Why? We are more than enough for them!"

"This is *not* our battle," reminded Valerian.

"And this is no place for a newfoundling." Under cover of his companions' wings, Taweel gathered the shivering angel child into his arms. "Fear not, Taji. I am Sent to you."

Clenched wings parted. "Overseer?" Taji asked tremulously.

Taweel whispered a promise in the boy's ear, then launched skyward, trusting the others to follow.

TRIED AND TRUE

Up and up, Taweel threaded his way through the stream of angels still circling the earth. Higher and higher, until only stars filled his view. Then he asked, "Are you hurt?"

Taji lifted his face and staunchly replied, "Only a little."

"Are you frightened?"

Taji hesitated, then quietly repeated, "Only a little."

Valerian pulled up nearby and curtly announced, "We are all here."

Scanning the hadarim of his encampment, Taweel said, "Fly high. And sing."

Dorum led out in song of thanksgiving, and Valerian got everyone moving in the right direction. Taking up the rear, Taweel gruffly said, "Show me."

239
Help is Near

In gentler tones, Taweel repeated, "Show me, Taji."

The boy plucked at the edge of a limp wing. "It hurts to move," he whimpered.

Slowing to a smooth glide, Taweel grimly assessed the damage. Somehow, an enemy dart had shattered, leaving dozens of slivers snagged in the sensitive inner folds of Taji's trembling wing.

Taweel's sympathetic groan was answered by a worried squeak. Lifting a hand to catch the little passenger riding atop his head, he asked, "Omri, can you help?"

With soft croons and delicate fingers, the yahavim set to work easing Taji's pain—one sliver at a time.

EMOTIONAL TURMOIL

Tamaes stayed in Taweel's wake all the way home. His mentor looked neither to the left or right as he strode through the encampment, not stopping until they were inside their own tent. Dropping onto his cot, Taweel resettled his wings around Taji before lifting his gaze to Tamaes's.

Pain. Regret. Anger. Doubt.

Tamaes touched his mentor's shoulder and whispered, "Well done, good and faithful."

Surprise. Gratitude. Peace. Weariness.

And then Dorum entered with Bern and Jacinto. He announced, "Valerian will bring a Caretaker."

Taweel nodded, then stiffened. His gaze snapped to Tamaes's face, and he asked, "Where is Adin?"

241
WITHOUT APOLOGY

"Right here." Adin stepped through the tent's entrance and leaned against his spear. "Did you need me?"

With a soft grunt, Taweel beckoned him over. "Do you have any injuries?"

"Scuffs and bruises. Nothing serious." Sitting beside Taweel on the cot, Adin leaned over and whispered, "Forgive me, Taji?"

The boy smiled sweetly. "You kept me safe."

"Only *after* I put you in danger." Adin's gaze locked with Taweel's. "Forgive me, Overseer?"

Taweel used his wings to pull him and Tamaes close. Taji giggled at the sudden crowding, but Taweel couldn't smile. Not with Gabriel's warning fresh in his mind.

Once Taji was safe in the hands of a Caretaker, Tamaes pried Taweel away, and they retreated to Loris's garden, where basins awaited.

"You're hurt!" Weft attacked Taweel's armor fastenings.

"It is nothing."

"Untrue." Tamaes grimly unwound his mentor's bootstraps. "Let us help."

Loris brought balm and bandages, and Omri pressed manna between Taweel's lips.

His injuries were miniscule. An aching wrist. A scored calf. Missing skin on two knuckles. Tamaes and Weft fussed overmuch, but Taweel submitted to their tender mercies with head bowed and eyes closed. Because a different pain pierced him deeply. And he needed their comfort.

243
CHILDPROOFING

In the shady alcove where they first met, Tamaes unburdened his heart. "I am afraid for Adin."

Taweel didn't seem surprised. "What changed?"

"My trust." Tamaes's wings shifted restlessly. "Why did you ask me to stay with him?"

"Valerian suggested it. And …."

"And?"

"Gabriel brought more than one message."

"What did he say?"

"After selection, our children will leave with their mentors, and this encampment will not welcome another newfoundling until …."

Tamaes's voice dropped to a whisper. "Until?"

"Until the danger passes."

With growing dread, Tamaes asked, "When will that be?"

Swallowing hard, Taweel said, "When Adin leaves."

Dorum met Taweel and Tamaes just outside the encampment. Catching sight of the bronze thread gleaming against eight new tunics, he asked, "Loris's handiwork?"

Taweel grunted.

"Selection?"

"In the next watch."

Dorum hummed. "That *would* explain our guest's arrival."

Tamaes asked, "Who?"

"Someone to lead our evensong."

With a soft gasp, Tamaes hurried ahead.

Holding Taweel back, Dorum said, "He arrived shortly after you left, and he made no mention of Selection."

Taweel's heart began to hammer, for a blue-haired angel stood with his arm linked through Adin's. "Asaph."

Dorum's voice dropped. "He says he came to hear Adin's song."

245
BACK ROW

Tamaes hung back, sitting beside Asaph's apprentice. Heartsick and silent, he watched eight youngsters scatter as their names appeared under their mentors' hands.

"Why do your wings weep?"

Glancing at the serious-faced teen in Worshiper's raiment, Tamaes said, "My mentor loves children."

"It shows."

Taweel's farewell song reverberated through the encampment, celebrating the new bonds being formed.

Tamaes explained, "We will not have more newfoundlings here."

Puzzlement put a crease between dark brows. "How do you know?"

Glancing in Adin's direction, Tamaes found his twin watching.

Adin winked and waved.

Tamaes dredged up an answering smile. "I will make sure."

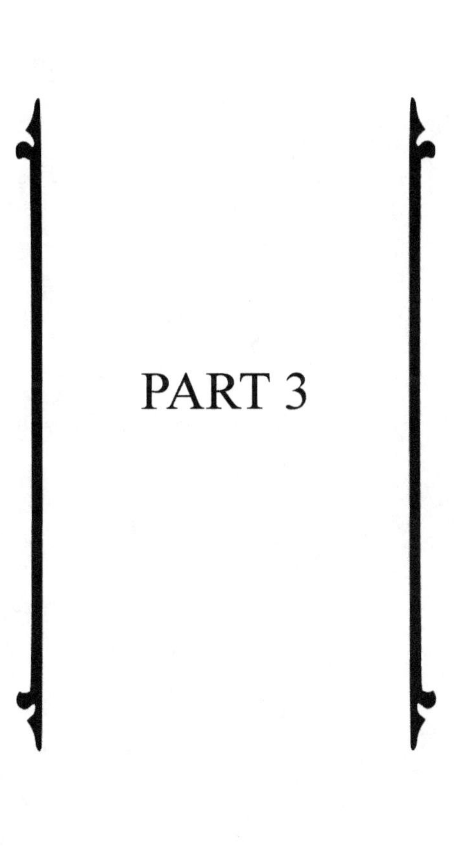

PART 3

CAPTURE THE FLAG

Young fighters swerved and strained, struggling to keep up with a swordsman whose flight path kept changing.

"Is he part Messenger?" muttered an adolescent.

"I heard he trains with them," panted his teammate.

"He's turned!" The leader of their training Flight cried, "Watch out!"

Bold as a cherub, blazing like flames, their lone opponent plunged through their ranks, scattering their formation.

A moment later, heavy boots hit the ground. Laughter sparkled in mahogany eyes as Tamaes claimed their banner and his victory.

"You made that look easy!" exclaimed a deep voice.

Tamaes turned to the silver-haired newcomer and blinked. "Taji?"

247
Passing Centuries

The training Flight swooped in, full of protests and questions, but Tamaes said, "A moment, please. This is my friend. Perhaps we can coax him into playing with us."

Interested gazes swung to Taji, who laughed. "Ages have passed, and I've come full circle. But this is wonderful! Are you a teacher, too?"

"No."

Taji roughed up short silver hair. In a lower voice, he asked, "You're still waiting?"

"I am."

"Is Taweel still overseer?"

"He is."

"I should let him know his new teacher has arrived." Taji patted the slingshot hanging from his sash. "Teacher ... and prospective mentor."

Tamaes slowly shook his head. "We have no newfoundlings."

"Yet. They arrive at regular intervals in every encampment."

"Not ours." Tamaes's jaw tightened. "I should take you to Taweel."

Taji fell in step. "It's strange. We were talking about you earlier."

"We?"

"Bern's thoughts often touch mine. He remembers our early days with great fondness."

"And Jacinto?"

Taji nodded. "We're closer than ever."

Tamaes felt so out of touch. If not for Taji's distinctive wing patterns, he wouldn't have even recognized him. "I have fallen short as your Fourfold brother."

"Now you'll be able to make up for lost time."

"How can this be?"

Taweel grunted. "Children grow."

"You've changed, too, Tamaes." A barrel-chested axeman propped an arm on his shoulder and leaned. "Just not as much!"

"Don't tease, Bern. Tamaes is the same." A swordsman with hyacinth curls stepped forward. "As is my admiration. Hello, brother."

Tamaes clasped Jacinto's hand and found he had to look up. With a jolt, he realized that Jacinto and Bern were pierced. "How can this be?" he repeated. But he wasn't talking about being the shortest warrior in the tent.

Taweel met his questioning glance and gruffly said, "You should check on Adin."

Tamaes found Adin near the bathing pools, struggling to bind a fresh wound. "What happened?"

Adin laughed lightly. "Don't ask."

"Let me." Tamaes knelt at his twin's side and straightened lopsided bandages. "Who wounded you?"

"Doesn't matter."

"Does Valerian know?"

Adin's eyebrows arched. "He's my mentor."

Which didn't answer the question. "You should not go into battle alone."

"Do you think so little of my skill?"

"I know your capabilities full well." Tamaes's mouth thinned. "Which is why I must wonder how you came by such a deep wound."

"Your concern warms my heart." Adin's smile widened. "But don't ask."

251
Don't Ask

Taweel found Tamaes sitting in a candle tree grove, boot laces unraveled, armor scattered on the ground. Dropping to one knee, Taweel asked, "Where are you injured?"

"Nowhere."

"Why did you remove your armor?"

"I feel helpless. Now I *am* helpless." Tamaes lifted mournful eyes. "Are there forbidden questions?"

"Ask me anything."

Tamaes struggled for composure. "Are apprentices ever Sent apart from their mentors?"

"Yes."

Surprise. Relief. Dismay. "Would you send *me* away?"

"I would. I will." Taweel took his trembling apprentice by the shoulders and spoke in soothing tones. "Not for good, but for your good. And not alone."

CHART A COURSE

"Let me lead," said Taji, whose golden wings blazed as they soared past star clusters and skimmed along the edges of vibrant nebula.

Jacinto asked, "Do you know the way?"

"Selection scattered us," reminded Bern. "Our mentors brought us to different forges."

Looping lazily around Tamaes, Taji boasted, "His star is my star, and its Fourfold are my friends."

"You *know* Nock?" asked Bern, sounding impressed.

Jacinto caught on. "You were Dorum's apprentice!"

Tamaes chuckled. "Yes. Taji's mentor was my mentor's mentor." Adding a burst of speed, he cheerfully called back, "But he cannot lead if he cannot keep up!"

253
ALWAYS CHANGING

Burnished feathers brushed along the ground as Nock approached the Forge's guests. He didn't stop until he grasped Tamaes by the forearms. "Much time has passed since your last visit."

With an answering grip, Tamaes smiled wryly. "I stopped growing."

Nock's brothers caught up. "Growth has little to do …"

" … with stature. You have …"

" … changed. And with each change …"

Baring his fangs, Nock's voice boomed as he finished, " … true friends will take your measure."

Taji cheerfully interrupted. "Are you taking volunteers?"

Tamaes turned to find him, Bern, and Jacinto with hands upraised.

No Easy Answer

"**W**hat's wrong?"

Tamaes winced as Taji tightened the bandages over a gash in his upper arm.

"Something's on your mind," Taji insisted. "Otherwise Bern wouldn't have been able to land a blow."

How could he answer? Tamaes knew something was wrong … or that something might go wrong. But in some vague hope that he was mistaken about Adin, Tamaes kept quiet. Instead, he said, "I do not understand why Taweel sent me away."

"Does the reason matter?"

"To me … yes."

Taji frowned. "Then why didn't you *ask* him?"

Tamaes quietly admitted, "Because I was afraid of the answer."

255
ALREADY GONE

Hidden within an opanim's whirling rings, Tamaes sang of longing—for his twin, for his mentor, for his charge. He ended with a renewal of trust. No matter how he was tried, he would remain true.

"Amen and amen!"

Tamaes recognized that voice!

Once the rings slowed enough, he leapt free, all but crashing into his mentor. Only there were tears in Taweel's eyes, and Tamaes panicked. "No!"

Taweel hauled him close. "Fear not."

"Adin!" Tamaes struggled free and begged, "Where is my brother?"

"He is already gone." Taweel's next words were heavy with relief. "Adin has finally been Sent."

Confusion robbed Tamaes of any joy he might have felt. "Adin has been Sent?" His hands shook, and he felt light-headed. "Is *that* all Gabriel meant?"

Taweel quietly said, "If only."

"You do not think so?"

"Do you?"

"No." With an aching heart, Tamaes said, "Adin has done much good. His skill is admired."

"And yet …?"

Tamaes hung his head. "I have tried to keep him safe."

"I know it. But you cannot stand guard over someone else's heart." Taweel set his fingertips against his apprentice's breastplate and solemnly said, "We are each responsible to God for our own."

257
Good Riddance

They met in dreams, and just like old times, Adin met Tamaes with a tackling embrace. "I win," he exulted.

"Were we racing?"

Adin shook his head, but his smirk begged to differ.

"Are you happy?" asked Tamaes.

He glanced over to see if Valerian or Taweel were listening. "Why has no one *ever* mentioned a gestation period?"

"A what?"

"Wait and see … and wait some more," Adin replied wisely.

"Are you happy?" Tamaes repeated.

"Deliriously." Adin punched his arm. "But why are *you* so happy? Glad to be rid of me?"

Tamaes relaxed into a genuine smile. "Never."

When Tamaes opened his eyes, Taji was standing guard. "Good news?" he asked.

"The best kind. Adin was Sent."

Taji brightened. "I remember when my turn came."

Tamaes sat forward. "You … you are not pierced."

"My joy is full."

A pang lurched through Tamaes's soul. "I want …."

"We all do." Taji shyly asked, "Would you like to hear? About her?"

"Please."

So he shared stories from the trove treasured up in his heart, whispering about a wisp of a girl whose faith was more beautiful than apple blossoms.

"Her name?" Tamaes asked.

Taji's smile widened. "Celia Mae Pomeroy."

259
STRANGELY SILENT

Taweel noticed right away, but Tamaes voiced his concern first. "Does it seem … quiet?"

"Unusually so," Taweel agreed, scanning the encampment.

Bern and Taji loosed their weapons, and Jacinto turned to walk backward. He asked, "Where is everyone?"

"Training?" suggested Tamaes. But the skies were empty.

The silence held a breathless quality, as if a storm might break. And then Omri peeped.

From within the overseer's tent came a muffled giggle.

Tamaes blinked. Taweel gasped. Trading wondering glances, they crept closer. Taweel slipped one finger between the folds of fabric, and Tamaes joined him in peering through the gap.

260
AMBUSH

Dorum and a copper-haired Caretaker sat with twenty-some newfoundlings. Stardust on lashes for newness. Fingers on lips for hushing. Twinkles in eyes for laughter.

Taweel slowly lowered himself to one knee.

"Have we surprised you?" Dorum inquired lightly.

Taweel's jaw worked, but no words came.

The Caretaker nudged several boys forward. "The gobsmacked one with the pixie accessory is your new minder. Take heart! You have him outnumbered!"

"My wings …." Taweel's throat closed. He lifted blurring eyes to Tamaes.

With a smile that was all fondness, he finished the welcome. "This is Taweel, and his wings are our shelter."

261
Share the Wealth

After evensong, Taweel sent Omri to find Tamaes. His apprentice soon ambled into view, tugged along by the little angel who had him by the hair. With a relaxed smile, Tamaes asked, "Am I summoned for assignment, song, or reprimand? Omri refuses to say."

Taweel huffed and rubbed his thumb over the black stone on his sword hilt. "Shall we look?"

"You have not checked?" Tamaes joined his mentor on the low garden wall. "I love this part."

"That is why I waited." With a musical scrape, Taweel slowly unsheathed his blade.

Tamaes whispered, "Twenty-two. We will need more tents."

Tamaes had always loved God's wordless writing. He touched the spirals of filigree swirling across the blade's surface, delicate as yahavim threads, whirling like galaxies. "If I flew far enough, do you think I would find my secret name written in stars?"

"A pleasant idea." Taweel flipped the sword over, and Omri flitted down for a closer look.

"Can you read them, Omri?" Tamaes asked.

The little angel gave the nearest whorl a pat, but if he knew, he wasn't telling.

Taweel slowly sheathed his blade. "We need common names, more tents, and raiment."

Tamaes's lips quirked. "We need Loris."

263
Oh, No

The changing of the watches found Taweel and Tamaes in the Weavers' District, where they startled a wispy boy with pale blue ringlets. "Oh, no!" he gasped, ducking out of sight.

Tamaes murmured, "Do you suppose …?"

Taweel grunted.

A small, six-fingered hand stole around the edge, and the boy peeped back out. Staring at their armor and swords, he asked, "A-are you lost?"

Tamaes spread his hands wide. "We are home."

All the boy managed was a tiny squeak, at which point Loris came to his rescue. "Peace, child." Beaming at the big Guardians, Loris explained, "My new apprentice."

By Increments

Little by little, Loris's apprentice grew accustomed to the comings and goings of warriors.

One by one, twenty-two young hadarim found their voices, their wings, and their confidence.

Bit by bit, Tamaes relaxed into the familiar pattern of work and worship … and waiting.

Only when his call came, it wasn't the one he expected.

"I need you!"

Tamaes shot to his feet as the ragged voice ripped through his mind. Desperation edged the next outcry.

"<u>He</u> needs you!"

Icy dread flooded Tamaes as Taweel rushed in, exclaiming, "Valerian …!"

"May we …?"

With a sigh, God's answer came. *'Go.'*

265
Hold Me Up

They plunged through a Caretaker's door, and heaven's light gave way to night and storm. Rain pelted, and wind sheered through narrow streets as the two Guardians hit the ground running. "This is the way!"

"Wait!" Taweel grabbed his apprentice's shoulder and raised his voice to be heard over the downpour. "Tamaes, wait!"

He obediently skidded to a halt. "But he needs me."

"So do I. Please, Tamaes. Help me." Taweel stepped closer and extended shaking wings around them. In their shelter, it was easier to hear the sound that was destroying Taweel's composure. Tiny hiccupping sobs. Omri was crying.

266
GRASPING AT HOPE

"Fear not. We are here." Tending to Omri took more seconds than Tamaes felt he could spare, but the yahavim was as dear as life to Taweel. By calming the sprite, Tamaes steadied his mentor. And perhaps in return, Taweel would be able to support him. "Does Omri know something we do not? Is it too late?" Tamaes asked shakily.

"Valerian called for help."

"Yes. He said Adin needs me."

"Then we are the help Valerian needs." From under the edge of a sheltering wing, Taweel peered through the storm. "We would not be here if there was no hope."

267
PIERCED THROUGH

Tamaes pointed. "I see something!"

A faint blur of green in the corner of an empty lot showed through the heavy veil of rain. Breaking into a run, Taweel called, "Valerian!"

"Here," came the coughing reply.

They found Adin's mentor sprawled amidst ragged weeds, the broken haft of a spear pinning his shoulder to the ground. Tamaes took a defensive stance while Taweel knelt in the mud and blood. "How did this happen?"

"Few could rival Adin in battle. Myself included."

Taweel groaned. "He turned on you?"

Valerian managed a brittle smile. "Let us instead say that I disarmed him."

From a Distance

"Courage," murmured Taweel.

Valerian rolled his eyes. "Likewise. Now do your part."

With a quick thrust, Taweel removed the spear from his comrade's shoulder. Quickly covering the deep wound with both hands, he said, "This needs a Caretaker."

"If so, then one will be Sent." Valerian pushed wet hair out of his eyes. "But I am your least concern. Go after him, Tamaes. Make him listen."

Tamaes hesitated. "Why would he listen to me?"

"Are you not his brother? The twin he cherishes?" Misery bled into Valerian's voice. "Adin never let me any closer than the point of his spear."

269
Back Up

Over the steady drum of rain, a growl reverberated. Tamaes wheeled, sword ready. "That wasn't thunder," he warned.

"Do not let the enemy delay you," snapped Taweel. "Go."

"No. You are outnumbered." Scuffling emanated from a murky alley along with a putrid stench. "My first responsibility is to you."

"Unless you are Sent," said a new voice. A barefoot angel stepped through a blaze of silver light. He glanced coolly at the sky, and the raindrops retreated as if in fear. "Which *they* are," continued the newcomer, casually pointing up as four angels dropped into the eye of the storm.

Bronze wingtips trailed, and hooves clattered against pavement. Taweel's heart sank, but Tamaes brightened. "Nock! Why are you here?"

"More to the point, why are you *still* here?" The silver-haired Caretaker eyed Tamaes. "Are you Sent?"

"I am."

"Then go."

Tamaes waited for Taweel's nod before rushing away, Omri darting after him.

Once he was out of earshot, Valerian stirred weakly. "He doesn't know."

"How could he? He rarely leaves the encampment."

The Caretaker interrupted again. "Make it quick, Guardian. Before he dims out."

Taweel gruffly asked, "What happened with Adin?"

"Same old story." Valerian's words slurred. "She died young."

271
COMPANION

Tamaes plunged back into the storm, wings arched against the cold slap of rain. Sword bared. Senses straining. But a series of shrill squeaks snagged his attention, and his tension shifted into disbelief as Omri smacked into his cheek and scrambled for a foothold.

"This is no place for you!"

Tamaes helped the little angel to his shoulder, where he lapsed into anxious whimpers. Slower now, but just as sure, Tamaes followed his Sending until his boot clipped a rusted grate that had once covered a vertical shaft. Chipped rim. Trickling filth. And dread.

"This is no place for any of us."

Ever since he was a boy, Tamaes had been leaping from heaven's threshold through a ring set in stone, but *this* hole ….

Why underground?

The possibilities only ranged from bad to worse. Hiding from the consequences of injuring Valerian. Injured and on the run. Snatched by the enemy. Tamaes refused to believe the worst. Hadn't Taweel gone rogue for a while? And he was the truest of angels.

"Are you crying because he's sad, too?" Tamaes asked.

Omri's uncertain chirrup wasn't very reassuring.

Jaw set, heart pounding, Tamaes leapt … and hoped his brother's path didn't lead to hell.

273
ℭLOSE QUARTERS

Tamaes hunched, trailing a hand along the curved ceiling as he shouldered past pipes. Light from his wings reflected off litter-clogged water and glinted in the eyes of skittering rats. He slowed as the tunnel emptied into a chamber where tunnels branched in several directions.

Stepping into the open, he waited for God to make clear which of the connecting passages he should follow. But no prompting came. "Adin?"

A faint shimmer caught Tamaes's eye, and he slowly crossed to the only other source of light. Cast-off raiment lay crumpled against the wall, half-hidden by the bodies of dead rats.

In the Dark

Strained creaks. Breathy keening. They were faint as the whisper of wings, barely audible above the gurgle and drip of water. But it was enough. With a soft click of his tongue, Tamaes warned Omri to stay put. He drew his wings around his shoulders and straightened. "I have been calling. Did you not hear me?"

"I always hear you."

Tamaes's heart leapt at the teasing lilt of his brother's voice. There were so many things he *wanted* to say, but he had been given a question. So Tamaes reached into the darkness and asked, "Adin, why are you hiding?"

275
COVERING

Amusement drenched Adin's tones. "I was naked, so I hid."

Tamaes glanced at the bunched raiment in his hand and reasoned, "You could cover yourself with your wings."

"Mine ache." He uncoiled from the shadows. "Will you hide me in the shelter of yours?"

"Of course." Tamaes propped his sword against the wall and beckoned with both hands. "But what of your mentor? *Valerian*'s wings should be your shelter."

"But you're here." Adin leaned into his brother and whispered, "Of course it would be you."

"Dress," Tamaes ordered.

Adin laughed hollowly. "Extinguish your light, and darkness will cover me anew."

276
SELF-APPOINTED

Adin complied, but with a mocking smile. "I've always hunted this way," he revealed. "Stealth is impossible when this stuff's radiance warns away my prey."

"I do not understand."

Orange light glinted in topaz eyes. "You knew I slipped away."

"Away," Tamaes acknowledged as uneasiness trembled through his shielding wings. "Into the fringes and enclaves. To train in other encampments."

"Into the lower places," Adin corrected. "To hunt down our enemy. To teach the Fallen fear."

Every part of Tamaes's soul rebelled against his twin's words. "We are hadarim. We were not made for such things."

"And yet I *excel*!"

"But we are Guardians. We *defend* life." Tamaes couldn't keep his gaze from straying to the dead rats piled in the corner.

"Defend, yes. But against *what*? We are warned that the enemy is vicious, blasphemous, and relentless, yet we tap spears with comrades in lofty encampments." A sneer twisted Adin's lips. "I *never* tasted danger during Valerian's sparring matches."

Tamaes's confusion deepened. How could his brother have wandered so far from what was truly important? Gripping Adin's arms, he gave him a shake. "But you were Sent. Should you not be with your charge?"

Adin's face slowly went blank.

Best and Brightest

Tamaes drew his wings more closely around Adin. "Brother?"

"Am I not skilled?"

"You are. No one in our encampment can disarm you. Even the enclave's cherubim call you formidable."

"I am!" Adin exclaimed, eyes flashing. "I became everything she could possibly need!"

She! There was such fierceness behind that single syllable. So Adin had been given a girl-child to love. Tamaes wryly pointed out, "We have both had ample time to prepare. Even still, I await my Sending."

"Waiting did not suit me, but it was preferable to this." Adin let his forehead rest against Tamaes's. "I was deceived."

279
CHEATED

Tiny creaks. A faint whine. Although the sounds whispered warnings, Tamaes pushed them aside in order to confront Adin's dismay. "Who deceived you?"

"I *loved* her." Adin's face twisted—pain, rage, disappointment. "He *made* me love her, and then He crushed my hopes. I did not wait millennia to be *wasted* on a life unlived!"

"Nothing is wasted," soothed Tamaes. "Your love will mark her existence for all eternity."

"Keep your false hope and lies!" Adin pushed away. "I'm better than this!"

Tamaes winced as a reedy note slipped off-key. Omri?

No. The sound was coming from Adin's furled wings.

"**Y**our wings," Tamaes whispered. "Show me your wings."

"Why?" Adin drew even further back and rubbed distractedly at one shoulder. "You've seen them often enough."

"But you said they ache." Tamaes used his own wings to gently corral his brother. "Unfurl."

Annoyance flickered across Adin's features. "*Don't* tell me what to do."

"But you could be injured."

"Like Valerian?" Adin continued to pull away. "Did you find him? Did he send you?"

"Taweel is with Valerian." Tamaes caught his brother's elbow. "You hurt him. Why?"

Adin's answer came soft as silk, heavy with warning. "He tried to stop me, too."

281
Blind Faith

Cold certainty gripped Tamaes's heart, and his hand fell away from Adin's arm.

For centuries, he'd helped teach young hadarim to be wise where the enemy is concerned. The mentors' warnings were always met with confusion. *How could they? Why would they?* Such betrayal was more than innocence could fathom.

Newfoundlings were naïve. Tamaes was not. But he'd always been a little slow on the uptake. Like a fool, he'd abandoned his sword and wrapped his only shelter around a newfallen.

"You have been blind." Adin smirked and looped his arms around Tamaes's neck. "Allow me to open your eyes."

THRILL OF THE HUNT

Omri clambered free of his hiding place and buzzed in tight circles, shrilling notes sharp as needles. Adin lunged and swatted the little angel to the ground.

Tamaes grabbed his wrist. "What are you *doing*?"

"Hunting."

"Not Omri!" Tamaes hauled Adin across the room and slammed him against the far wall. "I will not let you hurt him!"

"Too late." Prodding at the back of his head, Adin studied the dull smear on his fingers. "Far too late."

Swallowing thickly, Tamaes repeated, "I will *not* let you hurt him."

"Oh, brother." Adin chuckled darkly. "He's not the one I'm hunting."

283
My Brother's Keeper

Tamaes grappled with Adin, anxious to prevent him from getting anywhere near the limp splotch of light on the ground.

"Still worried about Taweel's tiny savior?" Adin asked mockingly. "Or were you hoping to be mine?"

Lowered gaze. Grim hold. Mute misery.

"You're here, and that's all that matters," said Adin. "You and I belong together."

"No."

"Do I mean so little to you?"

Tamaes struggled for words to explain his anguish. Staring into a face he knew better than his own, he choked out, "I have lost a brother."

"Not really." Adin smiled. "Because I'm going to keep you."

"N o."

"Where is your courage, warrior?" Adin countered. "Or do you still need to hold Taweel's hand for every little thing?"

"Yes." Tamaes fought back a sob, feeling more and more like a helpless child. "And I want him now more than ever."

Adin's smile vanished. "I will teach you regret."

"Because you already know it?"

Rage simmered in topaz eyes, and an odd noise stretched between them, like harp strings pulled too taut. An instant later, the darkness shattered around Tamaes, slicing his skin, catching his hair, lashing through the inner folds of his wings. And he was falling.

285
Broken Wings

When Tamaes's vision cleared, Adin was slumped over him. Shards, shreds, and spatters of luminous blood lay everywhere. Tamaes stirred, but moving made his wounds gush, so he went limp.

Adin's forehead rested on Tamaes's breastplate, and shudders wracked his body. "That *hurt*!" he hissed.

Long spines scrabbled along the floor, rattling as they dragged scraps of dimming glass through the muck. When Adin used them to push himself up, Tamaes realized. "You unfurled."

"*Don't* mock," Adin said through gritted teeth.

"Sorry," he whispered.

Adin's touch was unaccountably gentle as he inspected Tamaes's face. "Taweel is going to be furious."

"**Y**ou're in danger," Adin whispered, pressing his hands over a deep gash in Tamaes's arm.

"From you?" Noises filtered past the ringing in Tamaes's ears. Thunder? No, it was more like hoofbeats.

"Always." Adin's hands shook, but his voice was smooth. "We belong together."

"We did."

"Can you walk?" He glanced over his shoulder and grimaced. "We need to hurry."

Tamaes couldn't bring himself to fight his brother, but that didn't mean he would follow him. With a small shake of his head, he managed another, "Sorry."

"Liar." Adin kissed Tamaes's bloody cheek and whispered, "I will *make* you sorry."

287
GUARD AND GUARDIAN

"Taweel *will* be furious," Adin repeated. "But when he finds you gone, maybe he'll follow. We'll be together again."

Tamaes hardly knew how to respond to these impossible promises to drag him further into darkness. But he was spared from answering when Adin's hand clamped over his mouth.

"The hunters!" he snarled.

Adin was still shaky on his feet, but he lunged for Tamaes's sword, wheeling when a Fourfold exploded into the chamber. Hooves raised a din; bronzed feathers banished every shadow.

"Nock," Tamaes called weakly.

But Adin took a stand over him, exclaiming, "Fear not, brother! I'll protect you!"

"**B**e gone! He's mine!" The wings that had once been Adin's light and shield were now whip and thorn, barb and snare. Grinding fragments of his former glory underfoot, the newfallen angel fought with bared teeth and borrowed blade. "Tamaes would never abandon me!"

Nock and his brothers attempted to draw Adin away from his captive, but he held his own against the Fourfold.

From within the twisting cage of broken wings, Tamaes saw his mentor shoulder through the circle of bronze feathers. The look on Taweel's face was enough to prove Adin wrong. He wasn't furious. He was heartbroken.

289
EMPTY WORDS

Adin faltered at the sight of Taweel, which created the opening Nock and his brothers needed. They seized Adin, dragging him backward.

"It's not my fault, Taweel!" Adin struggled in their grasp. "I never meant to hurt him!"

Taweel silently plucked Tamaes's sword from Adin's hand.

"I know what you're not telling!" he accused. "About how your wings tremble in tune to the beat of one child's heart! How they rule you and ruin you!"

Taweel turned his back.

"Leave Tamaes to me, and he'll never be pierced!" Adin's voice hoarsened. "I'll save him!"

Still, Taweel spoke not a word.

NAMELESS

"What he said. Is it true?"

Taweel grunted. "Do not listen to the lies of the enemy."

Such finality. Tamaes struggled against the flat dismissal. "But he is *Adin*."

"He was." Taweel loosened his sash to bind another wound. "The Fallen do not keep their names."

Tamaes had always known this, but never had the truth given him such pain.

A sudden, terrible noise rang out—screech and roar, bawl and shout. And from the Fourfold's midst, their prisoner wailed his protest.

"Adin!" Tamaes gasped.

But a dreadful silence fell. They were gone.

Taweel's shoulders sagged. "He has been Cast."

291
HEALING HANDS

Recollection had Tamaes struggling to sit up. "Omri! I lost sight …!"

Taweel shushed him and released a tiny captive from within his wings. Omri burst free with an indignant squeak, which quickly turned to anxious crooning. Taweel explained, "He was badly hurt when he found me. The Caretaker who mended him …."

"… is here."

"Abner," Taweel greeted. "He needs you. Badly."

Tamaes stared dazedly into piercing gray eyes.

"Fear not," said Abner. "You'll soon be good as new."

Catching the Caretaker's sleeve, Tamaes begged, "Leave one. Please?"

Abner's eyebrows lifted. "Where?"

Tamaes touched the cheek Adin had kissed.

BY HIS OWN HAND

"Before my eyes," Valerian groaned.

Taweel grunted.

"How do you protect someone from their own folly?"

Without an answer, Taweel kept silent.

Valerian's captain passed the thorn-like blade. Abner led the encircling Flight in solemn chorus. Tamaes sank to his knees beside them, cradling Omri to his heart.

"Are you prepared?" Taweel murmured.

Valerian countered, "Are you?"

Taweel's hands shook, but his voice remained steady. "None can catch those who Fall. We can only be Faithful, trusting Him who is Faithful."

Twice-pierced, Valerian slumped against him and wept raggedly, and Taweel lifted his face, letting the rain take his tears.

293
THE FOURTH COT

Taweel and Tamaes flanked Valerian as they aimed for the Overseer's tent. Flowing cloth and four cots. Their home.

Outside, Valerian stopped short and stood so long, Taweel gripped his shoulder. "Fear not. We are with you."

"I know it." Briefly touching the second earring Taweel had bestowed, Valerian said, "I shall want my harp."

Tamaes quietly asked, "Would you like me to bring it?"

"Please." Dredging up a wan smile, Valerian admitted, "I do not think I can face that empty cot."

"I will go," Tamaes murmured, ducking through the opening.

But Adin's cot wasn't empty. Far from it.

Friend in Need

Asaph perched on the end of Adin's cot—hands folded, head bowed. Tamaes crashed to his knees before the blue-haired Worshiper and hid his face upon Asaph's lap. He couldn't stop shaking.

"Haven't you cried yet? Don't hold back on my account."

"Not here. Not yet." Tamaes's voice cracked. "You know?"

"That you need me? Yes. That you need to sing? Doubly so."

"Not *only* me."

"Collect Valerian's harp—and any keepsakes you and Taweel hold dear—and the three of you will follow me." Asaph's sleepy smile had a sad tilt. "The time has come again for next things."

295
FOREST GLADE

Tamaes lay limp—stripped of armor and barefoot in the soft grass. For the first time in his life, he'd sung himself to the point of exhaustion. No words remained, yet he wasn't empty. Nor was he alone.

Valerian pulled increasingly sweet cascades from his harp, and Taweel played with the flock of yahavim drawn in by Asaph's splendor. The Worshiper sang on in a solemn benediction.

A flicker of movement caught Tamaes's eye, and he turned his head. An adolescent Messenger with a riot of blond curls stood amidst the saplings. When Tamaes sat up, the newcomer hurried over.

The Messenger waved his hands. "Rest. Please. It sounds like you need it, after … everything."

Tamaes sagged back and closed his eyes. What did it matter if a passing Messenger overheard?

"I'm Milo, by the way."

Taweel grunted, and Tamaes cracked an eye. The Messenger had joined them. He sat quite close, his gaze expectant, as if waiting for something. An introduction? "I am Tamaes," he offered. "Apprentice to Taweel."

"I know." Milo smiled crookedly. "My mentor says I need to work on my timing. I like to fly fast, so I sometimes arrive earlier than I'm supposed to."

297
Renewed Vow

Taweel shot a look at Valerian, whose hands stilled against his harpstrings.

Do you think ...? Taweel couldn't finish the thought.

His friend slowly nodded. *The wait has been long.*

Closely watching his apprentice, Taweel waited for Asaph's song to resolve into silence. And in that moment where endings and beginnings touch, he saw Tamaes tremble.

Asaph turned. Omri peeped. Milo chuckled. Valerian hushed. Tamaes whimpered. And Taweel reacted as any mentor would. Strong arms for support. Bright wings for shelter. Gruff formality for a rite of passage long in coming. "Your call is my call. Our strength is doubled."

TENDERHEARTED

Eventually, every eye swung to the Messenger.

Milo sat with his chin on his fist, a gentle expression on his face, and a suspicious shine to his eyes. He sighed happily. "I'm going to *like* having Guardians around."

Taweel grunted. "Where is our Flight's tent?"

"We don't bother with one." Milo gestured to the surrounding glade. "For the angels of Jedrick's Flight, this is home."

Tamaes ventured, "And … my charge?"

"I'm here to guide you to your new family's home and Hedge." Milo stood and held out his hand to Tamaes, warmly adding, "I have good news for you."

299
FORLORN

aweel ached for Tamaes. Even Milo's good news had barely registered. Tamaes stood mute and marred in the farmhouse kitchen, so Taweel acted. Herding his apprentice into a corner, he sternly said, "You are ready for this."

"I disagree."

"You bring great skill and experience to this Hedge."

"*Your* skill. *Your* experience," Tamaes shook his head. "I am merely an apprentice."

"Only in name." Taweel gave him a small shake. "You outgrew your need of me long ago."

"No!" In a feat of strength that proved Taweel's point, Tamaes reversed their positions, pinning his mentor against the wall. "Stay mine."

"**I** am Taweel, mentor to Tamaes." His knuckles lightly rapped Tamaes's breastplate. "And my joy is full."

"But you are pierced."

"I am."

Tamaes tried to understand his mentor's reasoning. "Is it … the child? Do you share Milo's hopes?"

Taweel grunted. "Will the coming child be the beginning and end of your joy?"

He whispered, "No?"

"No," his mentor confirmed. "Joy comes from God, who gave you to me."

Hope trembled in Tamaes's weary heart. Different than he expected. Better.

Just then, Milo returned, leading a dark-skinned warrior with silver eyes. His slow smile warmed a single syllable. "Ah."

EPILOGUE
FLIGHT AND HEDGE

Taweel's heart ached to see Tamaes flounder. Every young hadarim faced this turning point with emotions running high, but not like this. Taweel's own Sending had been accompanied by giddy anticipation and awe. But Tamaes stood numbly before their new Hedgemate.

"Welcome. I am Lucan, apprentice to Othniel. God has given Naomi Pomeroy into my watch-care, and my joy is full."

In the silence that followed, Taweel studied the silver-eyed Guardian. Lucan wasn't one of the newfoundlings who'd passed through their encampment. Judging by the Weavers' notations on his raiment, he'd been newfound six centuries ago—old enough to exude confidence and competence, but still young in his eyes.

Taweel touched his apprentice's arm. *Shall I speak for us?*

A small headshake. A heavy swallow. "I am Tamaes, apprentice to Taweel. And this is Omri. We are Sent."

"Omri?" At Lucan's inquiring echo, the little angel squeaked from his place at Taweel's shoulder. "Ah. Hello, sweetling. You are welcome as well."

"Thank you," said Taweel.

Lucan's gaze rested briefly on the telltale embroidery on their raiment. Taweel doubted the Guardian could read it, but even an untrained eye could appreciate the abundance of Loris's handiwork.

"Your borders are as deep as Trumble's, and he is among the First," Lucan said.

"We are not, although my mentor was a First One," Taweel said, answering the implied question. "Is Trumble another Guardian in this Hedge?"

"Trumble is mentor to Jomei, who watches over Jayce Pomeroy." Looking to Tamaes, he added, "Father to the child you await."

Tamaes only nodded.

Lucan continued, "Trumble assigns the watches, but my mentor—Othniel—is

   Tried and True

considered the senior member of this Hedge. He has seen much." With another glance at the heavy borders on their raiment, Lucan said, "As have you …?"

Milo rushed to fill the awkward silence, touching Lucan's arm. "Save those songs for another evening. Tamaes recently lost a friend."

Compassion quenched the big warrior's curiosity, and his tones gentled further. "Do you have questions for me?"

Tamaes squared his shoulders and asked, "Where are the boundaries?"

Lucan slowly inclined his head. "We will walk them together. But do not hold back. You must be curious about your charge."

"Perhaps later," Tamaes said softly. Then he fled the confines of the farmhouse, Milo close on his heels.

Taweel sighed heavily, then bluntly shared, "Someone precious to us Fell. Give him time."

"Ah." Lucan gazed after Tamaes. "If God is willing, he shall have it. Nine months and more."

Tamaes walked in a straight line, past an herb garden with a bird bath, a tractor tire sandbox, and a lilac hedge in full bloom. He didn't stop until he found himself in a long aisle of apple trees. Blossom time was ending, so petals drifted from the branches. Tamaes's heart clenched painfully as he watched the tumbling petals land in the mud. Fallen. Broken. Scattered.

Mind locked on the image of Adin's ruined wings, Tamaes didn't realize he wasn't alone until a hand slipped into his. Milo was by his side, tears rolling down his cheeks.

"Why are you crying?" Tamaes asked.

The young Messenger pressed a hand over his heart. "Because you are."

And that was all. But the silence was less empty.

Even though this was his first brush with grief, Tamaes understood what he was facing. And that it wasn't wise to do so alone. His hand tightened around Milo's in a grateful squeeze.

When Taweel found them, he grunted and draped them both in his wings. "You are quick to befriend those of other orders," he murmured fondly.

　　　　TRIED AND TRUE

"Messengers are?" asked Milo.

"True, but I meant Tamaes." Taweel inclined his head in his apprentice's direction. "He mingles well for a hadarim."

Milo's eyes widened. "That's convenient!"

"In what sense?"

"Our Flight isn't exactly typical. We have Protectors, Observers, Caretakers, Messengers, and now you."

Tamaes mulled over the odd list. Cherubim and malakim were standard for Flights, as were the hadarim who required their support. But adahim were usually confined to towers, and samayim were rare.

Milo pointed into the sky. "Here's Jedrick now. Our captain."

The cherub's boots touched the ground a short distance away. Emerald wings rippled from his shoulders like a cloak as he came forward. "Taweel. Tamaes. Your names have come under my hand." With a faint smile, he added, "And your reputations precede you. My mentor trained in the enclave nearest your encampment. He spoke of you often and with great respect."

Taweel grunted.

"You *knew* Jedrick's mentor?" Milo asked.

Eyes skimming across the threads at their captain's collar, Taweel said, "Perth was newfound when we first met. Tamaes helped him hone his skill with the sword."

Milo goggled.

Tamaes shuffled his feet. "I am beginning to feel old."

"And I feel privileged." Jedrick drew his blade and showed them the blue stone set into its hilt. "My wings are yours, as is my sword. This Flight is your support, and I believe you will be ours. Are you familiar with those who serve as Grafts?"

Taweel said, "We are well-acquainted with two, though their service was centuries ago."

"Millennia," Tamaes quietly corrected.

Jedrick smiled ruefully. "Long before my time. And times have changed since then."

"The responsibilities of Guardian and Hedge remain the same," said Taweel.

"Amen and amen." But their captain shook his head. "You should acquaint yourself with the customs of this time and place."

Taweel inclined his head. "We will watch and

    TRIED AND TRUE

learn."

"I can offer better courses. Two of your teammates currently serve as Grafts." In tones of compassion, Jedrick said, "You have already met Abner."

Tamaes nodded mutely.

Milo jumped in. "The other one's my mentor, Harken."

"The Flight is scattered, but we will welcome you properly at evensong." Jedrick stepped back and nodded to someone behind them.

Tamaes glanced back, then *up*, for the Guardian waiting his turn was a veritable mountain of muscle with a shaggy mane of red hair.

Jedrick excused himself, saying, "When the time is right, Milo will show you the way."

Swords met with a metallic note that rang through Taweel's bones and sent his blood racing. This was battle. And he was glad. As the clash grew in speed and intensity, more angels gathered on the surrounding rooftops to watch Othniel test the mettle of their Hedge's newest Guardian.

"Few can keep up with Othniel," Lucan remarked.

Taweel could believe it. "Tamaes is not often challenged."

Milo's eyes were glued to the action. "Did he outmatch everyone?"

"We worked with children." Taweel waved at the sparring Guardians. "Warriors cannot test their limits while drilling the basics."

Lucan asked, "Do you spar like this with him?"

With a small shake of his head, Taweel explained, "After thousands of years and tens of thousands of matches, we know the dance too well. But there is no lack of skill in the heavens— returned hadarim, neighboring cherubim. And the occasional spar with a Fourfold."

"That would explain Othniel's delight," said Milo. "He's *enjoying* this!"

The Hedge leader grinned fiercely as Tamaes pressed an advantage, keeping Othniel from putting all his strength into his blows.

"Your arrival is truly a gift of God," agreed Lucan.

   TRIED AND TRUE

Taweel's gaze lingered on the hilts of the double swords showing over his shoulders. "Not many warriors are ambidextrous. Will you test your blades against mine?"

Lucan's eyes took on a shine. "As often as you like."

Tamaes sprawled on soft grass, gone limp in the aftermath of his training session with Othniel. The pleasant ache of tired muscles distracted him from deeper pains.

Overhead, a flock of yahavim swooped and reeled. From time to time, the little angels would pull together in a humming, glittering knot. Tamaes had never seen them act this way, and he found himself wishing he could ask Weft what they were up to.

"Comfort."

Turning his head, Tamaes considered the new arrival, a middling archivist with flaxen hair and a faraway look in his eyes.

He met Tamaes's questioning gaze and said, "They are holding up your friend."

"Omri?" He searched the tangle of activity for some sign of yellow hair, but it was no use. He was lost in their midst. Or perhaps he was found. Tamaes could still hear the sobs that had heralded Adin's fall. Perhaps Omri was equally heartbroken.

"I am called Ephron."

"Tamaes."

"Yes." The slim Observer joined Tamaes in the grass and said, "We are Flightmates."

"Has the time come for evensong?"

He shook his head, his gaze still fixed on the swirling yahavim. "I am early. I am Sent."

"To me?"

Ephron gave Tamaes his full attention—placid, peaceful, purposeful. "Yes. You know my order's role?"

"The adahim are the eyes and ears of heaven. My mentor and I spent several watches in one of your towers, telling the archivists about the things we'd seen."

A flicker of interest lit green eyes. "I would like to read that record."

"Or … we could talk." Tapping his breastplate, Tamaes said, "The stories are still here."

   TRIED AND TRUE

"I want to know you more." Ephron leaned closer. "And I am Sent to bear witness to a story that has ended."

Tamaes flinched.

Ephron waved slim hands. "Not here. Not now. Not yet."

"Adin Fell. Why would you want to hear about him?"

The Observer calmly asked, "How many of your memories of Adin are good?"

"Nearly all." Tamaes's chin quavered. "We were newfound together. We were rarely apart."

Sadness touched Ephron's smile. "Tell me about the friend you remember. Allow me to create a testament of the one you called brother."

Tamaes considered the offer. He'd already sung out his pain with Asaph, but this was different. Ephron was willing to collect a lifetime of brotherly love on the pages of a book. God loved Adin and wanted his memory kept.

Not the whine and crack of breaking wings. Not the sneers and snarls of accusation. Not the bitter regret and goodbye kiss. Tamaes couldn't have his twin back, but he would honor him. He would tell Ephron about boyish jostling and colliding embraces. Of clambering through the branches of candle-trees and having their hair woven into Weavers' crowns.

Catching Ephron's sleeve, he swallowed past the thickness in his throat. "He gave me my name. Adin called me 'twin' because we were brothers."

"Oh," Ephron breathed. "What a lovely way for a story to begin."

Weeks passed and Taweel was relieved that his apprentice had found outlets for his grief. Sparring with Othniel. Lengthy talks with Ephron. Games of chase with Milo. Tamaes didn't retreat into shadows, and his voice soared with the rest at evensong. But Taweel knew how things were meant to be.

Yes, they now served as part of a Flight. Yes, their strength had been added to a Hedge. But Tamaes was not Sent for their sakes. Taweel finally cornered and collared his apprentice, then dragged him into the framework of the small house under construction in the Pomeroys' yard.

     Tried and True

Tamaes ventured, "Have I earned a reprimand, my mentor?"

"You have done nothing wrong."

"Then why do your eyes accuse me?"

Taweel sighed. "Because this is not an encampment. Neither is it an enclave."

"I know it." Tamaes frowned slightly. "But we trained for this. Indeed, we trained others for this."

"You are a Guardian."

"Yes. And as a member of this Hedge, I stand guard through the watches."

"Over what?"

Tamaes's gaze dropped to the floor. "You know the perimeters as well as I do."

With a low growl, Taweel drove his fists into his apprentice's breastplate. "*Stop*!"

Reddish-brown eyes widened.

"You wanted me to teach you *this*." He pressed his knuckles into unyielding armor, anxious to reach the fragile heart underneath. "But now that we are here, you do not ask the one question that *should* be foremost in your mind."

Pain surfaced on Tamaes's face.

Taweel couldn't leave him like this. "You

have always confided in me. Please, Tamaes. Stay mine."

Trembling from head to toe, Tamaes whispered, "I am afraid."

"Of what?"

In broken tones, he repeated the words Adin had thrown into his face. "Will my wings tremble in tune to the beat of a human heart? What if they rule me and ruin me?"

Taweel groaned. "Nothing good comes of listening to the enemy's lies. You are not your brother. Fear not."

"Take my place?"

"We were made for this as surely as we were made for flight. I would never withhold this joy from you." Pulling Tamaes close, Taweel enfolded him in the shushing shelter of his wings. "We share this place. Fear not."

"I do not want to Fall."

"I will not let you Fall." Taweel set his hand on Tamaes's head, just as he'd done when he was small. "Now ask me the question that is foremost in your mind."

Tamaes whispered, "Is there a child for me?"

Taweel promised, "There will be."

 Tried and True

Tamaes reflexively lifted his wings to catch the young Guardian who skidded to a stop on the steep pitch of the farmhouse roof. Gideon sent him a wink before reporting, "They're packing up. We'll be in the orchard again this week."

Lucan unfurled. "You and Uri scout ahead with Trumble. Tamaes and I will follow with the family."

"See you there," Gideon said, tossing off a salute before doing a backflip off the edge of the roof. A moment later, he bolted straight up, then tucked into a steep dive. Leveling out, he swept close enough to the big tree in the front yard to ruffle its uppermost leaves with his fingertips.

At his sharp whistle, the angel posted on the machine shed raised an arm. Gideon met Uri's waiting hand, locking wrists as he hauled his mentor into the air.

"They are … unlike any other pair I have met," murmured Tamaes.

Lucan's gaze followed Gideon's progress. "How many have you known?"

"Thousands." Tamaes scratched idly at the

scar on the side of his face. "Many mentors brought their middling apprentices to Taweel."

"And to you."

"I was his support."

"And Gideon is Uri's." Lucan's slow smile made an appearance. "Their arrival brought both noise and stillness to our Hedge. At the next evensong, ask for their story. Gideon sings it well."

Summer had stretched into September, and by now, Tamaes was accustomed to this expectant family's habits. Until the completion of the second house, Jayce and Naomi were a household within a household, living under the same roof as Jayce's parents and younger sister. On Sunday afternoons when the weather allowed, the couple went into the orchard.

Lucan and Tamaes dropped to the yard as Jayce and Naomi left the house, carrying packs, bundles, and their boys.

"Nap?" asked three-year-old Tad. "Nap with daddy?"

"Sure, sure. We'll have a good rest under the trees."

"Duck! Duck!" exclaimed little Neil, who

　　　　　　　　Tried and True

was one-and-some and rarely still.

His mother sighed, "There he goes."

"I've got him," Jayce said, lengthening his stride to catch the errant toddler before he could make any more progress toward the duck pond.

Naomi called out, "Ducks in a row!"

Tad obediently trailed after his mother. Jayce set Neil on his shoulders and fell in step behind them, and Lucan and Tamaes brought up the rear. The pace was easy, with frequent stops as Tad chased grasshoppers in the long grass and picked dandelions for his mother. But eventually, they reached their usual spot, where Trumble, Uri, and Gideon already stood guard.

Draped screens and spread blankets. Toys, books, and favorite pillows. A tiny encampment.

The little ones quickly played themselves out, and Jayce called them back. Naomi rested on her side in the sun-dappled shade, patting Neil's back as he blinked drowsily at his collection of sticks. Tad hugged his favorite blanket—a quilt with apples, chickens, and tractors in the print.

Jayce grabbed a pillow and eased in behind the woman he clearly cherished. Tamaes was learning a great deal about family ties and faithful humans. Husband and wife. Parent and child. He moved to join Gideon and Trumble, who were sparring a few rows over, but his steps faltered.

A definite tug deep within made him turn back. What was this pull?

"He is praying." Lucan met his gaze from the other side of the blanket and clarified, "Jayce is praying for the child she carries."

Jayce had curled up behind Naomi, spooning her and splaying a hand over her stomach. Tamaes eased closer and knelt at the blanket's edge, spreading shivering wings over them.

Lucan nodded approvingly. "Prayer draws us near."

As Jayce sought God, Tamaes's wings steadied. With growing wonder, he realized that this father already loved a child he could neither touch nor see. Wasn't that the essence of faith?

Tamaes had been waiting for Taweel to teach him how to love his charge forever. But maybe his mentor wasn't the only one who could show the way. Because Jayce was way ahead of him.

 TRIED AND TRUE

While Naomi browsed through the bookshelves in The Curiosity Shop, Milo beckoned for Tamaes to join him in the back room. He felt incredibly awkward in the confines of Harken's shop. The shelves were too close together, the ceilings were too low, and there were far too many odds and ends just waiting to be bumped.

"Sorry. Only a little further," coaxed Milo. "We have one of Abner's doors here. The blue one."

Shuffling past stacks of books, Tamaes gratefully ducked through the ornate door and into their Flight's usual haven.

"Remember how Jedrick was saying we'd be gaining new members soon? Turns out *soon* is today!"

"I see." Tamaes lengthened his stride to keep up with the excited Messenger. Shifts in team make-up were common enough, but that didn't diminish his curiosity. "What order?"

"God Sent us two zamarim." Milo was practically skipping. "Abner should be done with them by now."

For a fleeting moment, Tamaes hoped he'd find Asaph waiting, but an unfamiliar voice carried through the trees.

"I haven't been this young since … ever!"

Abner blandly retorted, "You can finally act your age."

"Whoa, company!" As Milo and Tamaes arrived, a teenager with an abundance of red hair flung his arms wide. "What do you think? Totally me, right?"

Tamaes gazed into the upturned face of a scrawny teen with a telltale pattern of furled wings showing under the edges of his T-shirt. Jeans. Sneakers. Duffle bags. Instrument cases. They brought Tamaes to one startling conclusion. "You are a Graft."

"We *both* are." He pulled forward another teen who appeared to be roughly the same age. The resemblance ended there, for this boy had distinctly Asian features.

Since there was no sign of furled wings, Tamaes couldn't be sure how much Abner had altered his appearance. But he did know Taweel would be pleased. Resting his hands atop their heads, Tamaes said, "It will be nice to have young ones around again."

The Worshipers traded a look, and while

   TRIED AND TRUE

the dark-haired boy went to rummage in their baggage, the redhead stood his ground. "Why would you say that?"

"My mentor is fond of children."

His smile widened. "I'll totally let him fuss, but between you and me, Abner fiddled with my settings. I'm older than dirt."

"He's speaking quite literally," interjected Abner.

"This is *my* first undercover gig," said the second boy, who brought forward a blue electric guitar. Flipping it around, he showed Tamaes the name etched onto its back. "I'm enrolled as Levi Park. And though it's hard to tell, Myron here's my mentor."

"Hey, hey, hey! I thought we agreed I'm going by *Baird*."

As the truth registered, Tamaes let his hand fall away. "I apologize. I did not realize …."

"Why would you?" Baird grabbed his hand and got back under it. "As far as you're concerned, Myron Baird is a high schooler with a garage band and a total lack of parental supervision. You and your mentor can fuss and fond all you want. Seriously."

Tamaes dared to mess up a First One's hair.

Taweel liked the place God had prepared for them. He'd always enjoyed mingling with angels from other orders, and Jedrick's Flight now represented six. Although he and Tamaes were old enough to be considered ancient, three Guardians in their Hedge and two of their Flightmates were First Ones. Tamaes no longer complained about feeling old. Taweel *did* miss having newfoundlings about, but he and his apprentice would have a child to watch over soon enough.

Omri peeped in his ear.

"And you," Taweel said with gruff affection.

They found Tamaes on the roof of the apple barn, gazing out over the orchard. Moonlight gave the snowy landscape an eerie glow, as if the farm had been wrapped in raiment. Hunkering down beside his apprentice, he asked, "Do you have a question for me?"

This was Taweel's solution to Tamaes's long silences. A question a day. Tamaes usually had

     TRIED AND TRUE

one ready. Small matters, mostly. But tonight was different.

"Where do you think he was Cast?"

"Who can say? Far from here, I hope."

After a lengthy pause, Tamaes asked, "Is it wrong to love him?"

"I love him, too. God used you both to save me."

Tamaes gasped, and he turned to Taweel with a stricken expression. "*You* are hurt. Not once did I think …!"

Flame-hued wings unfurled and draped clumsily around Taweel's shoulders. With a soft grunt, he accepted the belated offer of comfort.

"Do you miss him?"

"Even more than I expected." Taweel stared into his empty hands. "We have new responsibilities and new companions. They fill the watches, but they cannot fill his place."

Tamaes shifted closer, so that their shoulders touched. Lowering his voice, he confessed, "I do not like his absence, but I am afraid of what he has become."

"Fear not." Meeting honesty with honesty, Taweel asked, "Do you think it is wrong that I loved you both, yet loved you more?”

“Is it wrong that I *wanted* to matter more?”

Taweel rested his hand on top of Tamaes’s head. “If he truly loved that little one, how could he think his life a waste?”

“Do you think he still loves us?”

This time, Taweel could offer an answer. “If he still harbors any attachment, it cannot be rightly called love. But back then, when he tried to take my apprentice from me, I hesitated. And so did he.”

“It hurts,” whispered Tamaes.

Taweel heard sorrow whispering through his apprentice’s wing and bowed his head. “It hurts.”

Tamaes had grown increasingly attached to Naomi Pomeroy. She was a smiling woman who sang as she worked—grateful, gracious, and given to hospitality. The beauty of her faith was a blessing to her entire family. And so seeing her in pain sapped the reserves of Tamaes’s courage.

Two nurses fluttered around trays of

   Tried and True

instruments as she groaned through another contraction.

"I do not understand how Lucan is still on his feet," said Tamaes.

Jomei shot him an amused look. "*This* time. After the fiasco surrounding Tad's birth, we learned our lesson."

"Othniel propped me up when Neil was born," Lucan calmly admitted.

"With Naomi's third child, her Guardian has finally found his feet," teased Jomei.

Lucan glanced away from his charge to study Tamaes's face. "Can you feel it? The time has come."

Jomei slipped over to Jayce's side and stretched wings that trembled in anticipation.

Pulse skittering on the verge of panic, Tamaes shuffled forward. But he didn't know what he was supposed to *do*. There was no enemy here, no reason to draw his sword. And he was keenly aware of the fragility of life. What if something went wrong? Would he blame himself? Would he blame God?

Part of Tamaes wanted to flee the hospital room, but Jayce's prayers held him there … and urged him nearer.

"That's it. Nice and steady," the doctor coached. "Deep breath, Naomi. One more push."

Taweel stepped to Tamaes's side, one strong hand locking around his apprentice's arm. When Tamaes flung him a desperate look, his mentor actually smiled. "Deep breath, Tamaes."

He dragged in air. Naomi pushed. The doctor sounded pleased. Jayce's laugh sounded a little soggy. And a thin wail made it past the ringing in Tamaes's ears.

'This is a good gift,' declared his Maker. *'Cherish her.'*

Tamaes swayed under the heavy burden of God's joy. He sought his mentor's gaze and found it waiting. Purple eyes were alight in a way Tamaes had never seen before.

A girl.

Tamaes hoped Taweel knew what was supposed to happen next.

Clearly he did, because when Tamaes collapsed, it was into his mentor's waiting arms.

He woke to the stirring of notes, indelible in their sweetness. Opening his eyes, Tamaes quickly shut them again. "I apologize."

"No need." Taweel loosened his hold, though the folds of his wing still cosseted him. "The others have gone to the roof. You and I remain on guard."

"I fainted?"

"You fainted."

Tamaes sighed and reopened his eyes. They were sprawled together on the floor, with Taweel serving as his backrest. The hush of night and sleep surrounded the maternity ward. A welcome change after the confusion of labor and delivery.

The whisper of music came again, and this time Tamaes realized where it was coming from. Taweel's wings. The one not wrapped around him arched over a plastic cradle, and its song was a lullaby of love.

"Do you want to see her?"

Tamaes shook his head. He didn't feel ready.

Huffing in amusement, Taweel asked, "Are you content to leave your charge under Omri's watch-care?"

Curious now, Tamaes pushed up onto his

knees so he could see over the edge of the small bed. Taweel knelt beside him, wings widespread, expression peaceful.

A swaddled baby slept in the cradle, blonde fuzz peeping out from under a snug pink hat. Omri sat cross-legged beside her, humming softly as he gently threaded his fingers through the tuft of hair.

"Are you pleased, Omri?" asked Tamaes.

Faceted eyes blinked up at them, and the little angel offered a crooning trill.

Tamaes cast a shy glance at the bed where Naomi slept, then carefully reached into the crib. Almost at once, he hesitated. Big, rough, and browned—his hand was larger than his charge. Tamaes felt over-sized, yet pleased that he had been made strong for her sake.

He brushed a fingertip across that wisp of hair, then grazed her fair cheek with one knuckle. His breath caught at the strength of the emotions that surged through his soul—possessiveness, protectiveness, and ... *oh*. Tamaes blinked to clear his vision. "This."

Taweel sighed happily. "This."

Omri's *peep* made it unanimous.

 TRIED AND TRUE

Reaching for the sword that rested next to his own, Taweel offered it to Tamaes. "This is my favorite part."

Turning their backs on the wee bed, they sat on the floor, heads bent together as Tamaes slowly released the blade from its sheath. Etched deep into the gleaming metal, amidst delicate filigree and whorls, God had written a name—*Priscilla Mae Pomeroy.*

About the Author

Behind the scenes, I'm a cheerful homebody whose many talents include dish-washing, laundry-sorting, and the weaving polysyllabic words into everyday conversation. First to know, last to tell, happy to try, and always true. A plotter and a plodder, a dabbler and a devotee. Weaknesses include bright colors, crazy socks, and alliteration. More to the point, I spend my days planning studies, plotting stories, and putting my nose to the proverbial grindstone … because as much as I loves writing, it's work. Finding the perfect word, turning a phrase so it sparkles, giving a plot just a bit of a twist—they're worth every iota of effort. I'm delighted to have discovered what I want to do when I grow up!

Christa also publishes family-friendly fantasy under her maiden name. If you like magical master sculptors, shape-shifting brothers, stowaways with secrets, and mythical creatures, let your curiosity lead you to CJMilbrandt.com.

Threshold Series art, outtakes, and postcards await you on Christa's website. Be sture to drop in for milestone parties, character Q&A sessions, and news about upcoming and ongoing stories.

ChristaKinde.com

Facebook /ChristaKinde

Pinterest /christakinde

Twitter @ChristaKinde

ALSO BY
CHRISTA KINDE

THRESHOLD SERIES

The Blue Door (Book 1)
The Hidden Deep (Book 2)
The Broken Window (Book 3)
The Garden Gate (Book 4)

THRESHOLD COMPANION STORIES

Angels All Around
Angels in Harmony
Angels on Guard
Angel on High
Angel Unaware
Rough and Tumble
Tried and True
Sage and Song

POMEROY FAMILY LEGACY COLLECTION

Pursuing Prissie
Sweets for the Sweet

*Angels: A 90-Day Devotional
about God's Messengers*

9 781631 230400